The Sleeping Army

by the same author

FRANCESCA SIMON

The Sleeping Army

P

PROFILE BOOKS

ff

faber and faber

First published in 2011
by Faber and Faber Limited
Bloomsbury House,
74–77 Great Russell Street,
London WC1B 3DA
and
Profile Books Ltd
3A Exmouth House
Pine Street
London EC1R 0JH

Typeset by Faber and Faber
Printed in England by Clays, Bungay, Suffolk

A CIP record for this book
is available from the British Library

ISBN 978–1–846–68278–0

4 6 8 10 9 7 5 3

For Steven Butler and Emily Woof

. . . The gods die,
or never lived. They crawl home, damp and slow,
to the subtle, shallow sea that made them.

Emma Jones, 'Daphne', *The Striped World*

Contents

What if Christianity didn't exist? What if people still worshipped the old Norse and Anglo-Saxon Gods . . .

1 The British Museum

'Gods damn you!'

Freya's father held the phone away from his ear as her mother continued screaming. 'Why are you so useless? Why can't you get anything right?'

'I'm sorry, Clare, I messed up, I'll sort—'

'You have Freya on Thorsday nights, every Thorsday night, how hard is that to remember? It's a school night, and you've dragged her into work—'

Freya stopped listening. Her father's shoulders, in his too-tight black uniform, tensed up to his ears.

She felt sorry for him. It didn't seem right, somehow,

to feel sorry for your father. Clare, her mother, so efficient, so competent, and her father, working nights now as a security guard at the British Museum since he'd lost his office job. He'd changed shifts, and forgotten he had her on Thorsdays not Wodnesdays now, and every other weekend.

It was funny, her mother was always preaching to her throng to follow the gentle Baldr's example yet the moment she spoke to Freya's dad all her soft words deserted her and she became a demented troll.

Her father hung up. 'Sorry,' he said. 'Sorry. Sorry. Sorry.'

Freya wished he'd stop apologising all the time.

'It's okay,' said Freya. 'I like being here.'

It wasn't okay, but she did like being in the museum. She'd never been here at night before, and it made her feel special. The cool, quiet rooms were all hers now.

In the daytime, it was so crowded with tourists clustering round the armour, or the Rosetta Stone, or that creepy human sacrifice from the Lindow peat bog garrotted by heathens long ago that it was hard to actually see anything. Especially if you weren't very tall. Clare used to bring her all the time when she was young. Once a guard had called her a little Loki when she'd tried to climb up the giant marble statue of Thor

2

guarding the entrance. Freya shivered. She hated being told off.

'My boss knows you're here,' said Bob. 'She's not happy, but she's got kids, too, and I told her what a good girl you were. Just wait here for a sec, while I sign in. I'm patrolling the upper floors tonight.'

'What's up there?' asked Freya.

'Wodenism in Medieval Europe. Aztecs. Japan.'

'Oh.'

Freya had hoped he'd be with the Egyptian mummies, or even the Ancient Greeks. Bob saw her face.

'I know I've made a mess of things, Freya, and I'm sorry, I'm sorry, I'll make it up to you, next time you come over we'll do whatever you want, your choice.'

'It's fine, Dad,' said Freya. 'Really.' She was an only child, and used to trying to make things better.

Freya ambled about the Great Court, enjoying the sound of her feet slapping against the white marble floor. Just for fun she walked all the way round the old circular library, reading the inscription carved on the top of the wall:

QUEEN ELIZABETH II AW 5000. THIS GREAT COURT CELEBRATING THE NEW MILLENNIUM IS DEDICATED TO HER MAJESTY.

Freya was one of those people who read anything with writing on it. Cereal packets, bus adverts, graffiti. To kill time she read all the banners, gnawing absentmindedly on her fraying sleeve.

There were posters announcing the forthcoming exhibition of Italian drawings, including the sketches for Leonardo da Vinci's famous painting of Woden feasting with his warriors at the last supper in Valhalla before Ragnarok. Freya yawned. The African masks looked a lot more exciting.

She sat down to wait for her dad at the base of a tall lump of carved stone. Idly, she read the inscription:

Anglo-Saxon sandstone hammer shaft. Late 38th to early 39th century AW. Hammers such as this stood as powerful images of the Wodenic faith in Anglo-Saxon England.

Freya yawned again. She'd had PE today, which she hated. She stopped herself from leaning back against the stone with a jerk and looked around to make sure no one had noticed.

'Right, Freya,' said her dad, pulling on his black fleece jacket embroidered with the white British Museum logo. 'Heave your bones. And stop chewing on your sleeve.'

Freya sighed. Not so loudly that Bob would tell her off, just loud enough so that he knew she wasn't happy. Then she followed him up the great staircase, flanked by the marble mausoleum lions, counting the stairs as she went. She knew there were sixty, but she liked counting them just the same.

'What's Ragnarok?' asked Freya.

'Don't they teach you anything in that Fane school?' said Bob.

'No,' said Freya.

Her dad grinned.

'It's the day when the world ends and the Gods die in a great battle,' said Bob. 'The prophet Snorri Sturluson called it the *Twilight of the Gods*. It's fascinating that—'

'Got it, Dad, thanks,' said Freya. Bob had a way of going on and on whenever you were dumb enough to ask him a question.

They reached the top of the stairs and entered the large foyer. Everything was dark and still. The exhibition cases were little pools of light in the surrounding darkness. The gold helmets and treasure from the Northumbrian hoard gleamed dully. It was actually a little spooky, all these old bits and pieces.

Bob turned off the foyer into Room 40. Next door she

5

could hear the clocks sounding their out-of-time bongs.

Freya looked around. She'd never been here before.

This room is dedicated to exploring the spread of Wodenism as a major religion throughout Europe and the heathen cults which preceded it.

And that of course was why she'd never been here before. Freya sighed loudly.

'Freya, listen to me,' said her dad, switching on his flashlight. 'Don't leave this room or you could set off an alarm. There's a chair in the corner you can sit on to do your homework. If you get tired we can chuck you in a sarcophagus with a pillow.'

'Ha ha,' said Freya.

'Here, have some chocolate,' he added, handing her a KitKat. 'And take a look at that display of medieval silver chalices from Woden's shrine at York,' he called over his shoulder. 'Very exciting.'

Freya put the chocolate in her pocket, and obediently bent over the display case.

This silver gilt cup is a rare survival of a fine English chalice and was designed for ceremonial use on Woden's Feast Days.

'Oh, Hel,' muttered Freya under her breath. She made a face. She got enough religion at home with her mother, thank you very much.

Sometimes it was embarrassing being religious. Even though the Queen was head of the Fane of England, and Britain was a Wodenic country, not everyone believed in the Gods any more. Baby-namings were still popular, and swearing on Thor's sacred oath-ring of course, but apart from that the Fanes weren't exactly bursting at the seams. The Archpriest of York had devoted his *Thought for the Day* on BBC Radio 4 this morning to criticising people for their lacklustre religious observance. Freya had had to listen to him droning on while she was eating her cornflakes.

Not that this was a subject Freya could discuss with her mum. Just last Sunday Clare, looking splendid in her long white robes, had been railing from her altar against atheists like Richard Dawkins for his book, *The Gods Delusion*, and had forbidden Freya from even looking at it. 'Remember, Freya, there are no atheists on aeroplanes,' Mum liked to say.

'But no one's ever *seen* the Gods,' said Freya once. 'So how do we know they exist?'

'We don't see the Gods any more because we're bad,' said Mum. 'Long ago they used to walk among us.'

'Dad doesn't think they exist,' said Freya boldly.

Clare pursed her mouth. 'Your father is an idiot. Don't get me started.' And she'd gone to the phone to drum up volunteers for her neglected altars scheme, to maintain the crossroads shrines.

Freya sighed. Just her bad fate to have divorced parents. When she needed her gym kit it was at Mum's. When she wanted the book she was reading it was at Dad's. It felt like everything and everyone was always in the wrong place. Especially her.

She played with the little gold hammer hanging round her neck which Mum had given her on her confirmation day when she'd chosen Thor for her own protector God. The fifth commandment, *Honour your children, for they alone will remember your name*, was inscribed in tiny letters along the shaft. Shame her parents didn't recall that more often, thought Freya. Especially around birthday time.

It was her bad fate to have been born on December 25th, the same day as Woden's Feast Day, which meant she always got combined birthday/feast day presents, even though her parents both swore this wasn't true. But it so was.

Bob popped his head round. 'You okay, hon?'

'Fine, fine,' said Freya, pretending to be getting on with

8

her history homework (*Henry VIII broke with the Lord High Priest of Copenhagen and established the Fane of England in 4534. What were the reasons?*). Freya longed to write, 'Because he was bored and hated marzipan,' but didn't dare.

Grrrr. Aaaarrrghhh. She could sit, wailing and gnashing and bemoaning her cruel fate, or wander the room wailing and gnashing and bemoaning her cruel fate. Grimly, she opted for wandering. She would look at every stupid helmet fragment and bent old spoon and read every stupid description. Anything to avoid getting down to work on her stupid, boring essay.

Freya stood, stretched, and stomped over to the small display case tucked into the right-hand corner. She peered through the glass at two round, earth-red medallions.

Seated woman with baby on her lap. Donkey looking on.

Man hanging on decorated cross.

Found in the catacombs, Rome, around 3300 AW. Sacred objects from the Christian cult, one of the many exotic religious cults in the Roman Empire which sprang up as the empire expanded eastwards.

Suffered intense persecution and died out by the
end of the 34th century AW.

Freya turned away and skidded on a creased piece
of paper on the floor. I could have really hurt myself,
she thought crossly, picking it up and smoothing the
dirty folds. It was a partially-filled-in 'Family Fun
Worksheet', the kind Bob was always trying to get her
to do whenever they came to the museum.

Discover Long-Ago Religions!

Can you imagine how different modern Britain would be
if ancient religions like Roman Christianity or Egyptian
Amunism were practised here?

Now pretend that people in Britain worshipped the
Christian god (called Christ) instead of Woden, Thor, Sif,
Freyja, Tyr, Baldr, and all our other Gods. What would be
different?

We'd worship _one god_ instead of many.

We'd be called _Christians_ instead of Wodenists.

Our sacred book would be the _Gospel_ instead
of the Edda.

Our sacred symbol would be a ~~donkey? pomegranate?~~ cross
instead of Thor's hammer.

Our places of worship would be called <u>Churches</u>
instead of Fanes or Temples.

Can **YOU** think of any other differences?

Yes, thought Freya. I wouldn't be stuck here writing
about stupid, fat old Henry VIII.

Now imagine Britons worshipped the ancient Egyptian
gods like Osiris and Horus and Isis and Amun-Ra.

Our most important god would be _____ instead
of Woden.

Freya crumpled up the worksheet and dropped it
back on the floor. Then she felt guilty for littering,
picked it up, and stuffed it in her schoolbag. She'd put
it in the recycling bin when she got home.

The next case exhibited axes and knives used in
the long-ago days when humans and animals were
sacrificed to Woden. Ugh. No one really liked talking
about *that*.

In the centre of the room was a large display case
containing several creamy ivory chessmen. Freya peered
at the pale, golden-brown figures.

**67 ancient chess pieces, found partly hidden in a
sandbank on the Scottish island of Lewis.**

Their origins, how they came to be buried, and why there are so many 'extra' pieces are shrouded in mystery. Displayed here are eight queens, eight kings, fifteen knights . . .

Freya stopped reading and gazed at the chessmen. They looked weary and glum, with bulging, startled eyes, frowning mouths, and hunched shoulders. Some of them appeared positively disgruntled. Mostly they looked sad, as if something terrible had happened, something they were helpless to do anything about except brood for eternity. The sorrowful queens looked a lot like Clare did sometimes, late at night when she thought Freya wasn't looking, after she'd just been on the phone with a depressed member of her throng.

Wonder what they're so worried about, thought Freya. She especially liked the ferocious-looking berserks, the ancient warriors sacred to Woden, biting their shields with their big teeth. Those fearless, terrifying soldiers, who went into a battle frenzy and fought like wild animals, impervious to pain, had always fascinated her. She'd seen pictures of berserks in primary school, and they'd had a fun day dressing up and running around snarling and attacking each other. But the rows and rows of pawns looked like tombstones. She shuddered.

And then there it was, resting on an open stand behind the Lewis chess pieces, like an offering. The carved ivory horn, decorated with enamelled silver panels inset with green jewels, dangled from the ceiling on two ornate chains. Runic inscriptions circled the wide bell. Freya went over and peered inside. She couldn't see from one end to the other. The curved horn was enormous, bigger than she was.

Ceremonial horn from a Viking silver hoard. Origin unknown.

The urge to touch it was overwhelming and irresistible.

Freya glanced around. No one could sneak up on her, not the way footsteps creaked on these wood floors. Slowly, she reached out and brushed the wide-brimmed bell of the horn with her fingertips. The ivory was ridged but velvety-smooth. She jerked her hand back quickly, waiting for an alarm to sound and guards to come running and throw her into prison. But no alarm sounded.

Freya circled it again and stopped before the ornate

tip. Hypnotised, Freya stood on tiptoe, put her lips around the horn's narrow mouthpiece and blew.

A thunderous roaring ringing shrieking blast rumbled and swelled, pealing and blaring louder and louder and louder until Freya didn't know where her body ended and the sound began.

Freya jerked her mouth away but the ringing horn blasts continued reverberating. The roaring, swelling earthquake exploded around her, clap upon clap of thunder, pealing, clanging, booming, banging, booming, banging, booming, banging until she thought her head would split.

She pressed her hands against her ears but the blasts were inside her now, controlling her heart, her breath, her life's blood.

The white carved ceiling and walls cracked and a gigantic gash zigzagged across the floor. Armour and shields crashed from the walls while all around her was the sickening sound of smashing pottery and glass. Every alarm in the museum went off.

There was a humming in her ears. A feeling as if the moving air was cracking and thinning then thickening around her. There was an overpowering smell of frost and fur. She felt as if her body were breaking apart.

The air hissed and bubbled, splintering into shards

of ice. The glass case containing the Lewis Chessmen shattered. Freya was caught up in an icy whirlwind, like a wave snatching her ankles and spinning her through space.

Bob, running into the room shouting her name, glimpsed a queen. A king. A berserk. A riderless horse. And Freya, spiralling together through the air, sucked into a vortex of flashing lights.

Then they vanished.

'Freya!' he screamed, stumbling as he crunched through the ivory pieces and glass scattered across the floor. He stood in front of the smashed display case and buried his face in his hands.

Oh Gods, he thought. Oh Gods. Clare will kill me.

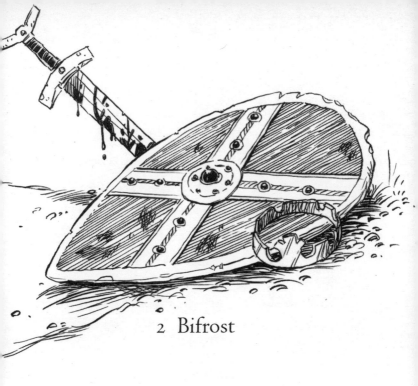

2 Bifrost

Ow. Something sharp was jabbing her in the ribs.

'Get off me,' mumbled Freya, pushing feebly. She felt dizzy, as if she'd been punched in the stomach.

Someone beside her was screaming. Freya heard the harsh, angry words, rasped out in a language she couldn't understand.

'What?' she whispered.

'Get your fat elbow out of my face!' snapped a girl's voice. 'And get your filthy hands off my crown.'

Had there been an earthquake? Freya seemed to be trapped under a twisted pile of struggling bodies.

There was a terrible rank smell of dead animal.

Whoever was on top of her rolled off. Freya sat up. Her head was swimming. Dimly she heard traffic noises. She was lying in the middle of the road, in a knotted tangle of arms and legs and clothes. A girl and boy, both wearing crowns and knee-length fur tunics, struggled to their feet beside her. Their legs were trembling. The girl-queen wobbled and fell over. The boy-king took a step and collapsed to his knees, his slender sword clattering to the ground.

Somehow she was outside. How had she got here? She looked up and saw a horse. A huge grey horse with eight legs, dancing nervously, its hooves thrumming the cobblestones, striking fire.

She was hallucinating. Woden's priestesses went into trances sometimes after pouring wine on an altar. (The High Fane ones still used ox-blood – yuck.) Maybe this was a trance. A strange trance, hearing honking cars, seeing the lights of Woden's domed Temple lit up in the London night sky and a horse with eight legs.

Uhh, thought Freya, this is some strange random dream. Maybe I'm in hospital. Or maybe I'm dead, and this is Hel. Freya shivered. It was certainly cold enough to be Hel.

Freya saw twin light beams coming towards her. Headlights. Car headlights.

I have to move, she thought. I really have to move. But somehow that seemed too much effort.

'Get up! Run! Now!' yelled the boy. He yanked her to her feet. 'Now. On to the bridge! Now! Run!'

'RAAAAAAA!' A giant man wearing a bear skin, sword outstretched, raven shield raised, charged straight at her, snarling and roaring like a frenzied beast. Foam dripped from his mouth.

Freya screamed.

The crazed creature hurtled past her towards an oncoming car, bellowing and shrieking. The car screeched to a halt. Its windscreen shattered as the Bear-Man plunged his sword through the glass.

Cars slammed on their brakes. Freya heard a terrible howling as the Bear-Man attacked another car. Then screams.

She turned. The Bear-Man was surrounded by cars.

'We can't—' stuttered Freya.

'Leave him!' ordered the boy. 'He's a berserk. He's crazy. We can't wait.'

'Bear-Shirt!' shouted the girl. 'We've got to get on to the bridge!'

'Shut up, Roskva! Save yourself,' said the boy.

'Don't tell me to shut up, you stupid troll!' screamed the girl, adding a few more harsh words in her strange language.

Suddenly Freya knew where she was. On Upper Thames Street by the wobbly Millennium Bridge. The Tate Modern was straight ahead. Clare had taken her there only last week to see the Salvador Dali lobster phone.

The boy-king grabbed Freya's hand. The girl-queen grabbed her other hand and the horse's bridle. Half-running, half-dragging her, they sped along the pedestrian passageway between the City of London School for Boys and the headquarters of the Asgard Army. They moved incredibly fast. Everyone heading in their direction stopped and gaped. Someone started taking pictures. 'I'm telling you, the horse has eight legs,' gabbled a woman into her mobile.

'Where are we going? Where are you taking me?' screamed Freya.

'Shut up!' said the girl.

'We have to get on to Bifrost before it vanishes,' said the boy.

'Bifrost?' said Freya. '*Bifrost?* But that's—'

They were racing across the wobbly bridge towards the dark hulk of the Tate Modern, their feet clinking on the metal surface, when she saw the flaming, three-coloured rainbow. It curved out of the night sky lower than any rainbow Freya had ever seen, the bottom edge hovering over the middle of the Millennium Bridge. The rainbow shimmered, reddish-yellow, greenish-blue. Flames shot into the sky from the red band at the top, reflecting in the dark water of the Thames. A rainbow at night? thought Freya. A rainbow on fire? What's happening to me? The other pedestrians hurried past, unseeing.

'Jump on!' said the long-haired blond boy, pushing her. 'There's no time to lose.'

'Where are we going?'

'Asgard.'

Freya stopped dead.

'Asgard? The Realm of the Gods?' said Freya. This was definitely the strangest dream she'd ever had. She made the sign of the hammer. 'Thor protect me, Thor protect me,' she whispered over and over.

'No, Asgard, Iceland,' snapped the freckle-faced queen. 'Asgard, Sweden. Asgard. Asgard. Where else does Bifrost lead?' She jabbed Freya hard in the back. 'Jump!'

Freya jumped. She was too scared and too shocked to resist.

The dazzling, flaming bridge wobbled beneath her. Freya swayed, then steadied herself as her feet sank into the shimmering road. She kept well away from the flames rising from the edge. Behind her the horse's eight hooves chimed on the gleaming surface.

She took one step, and then another. It was like walking on blue-green sand. She was on Bifrost, the trembling rainbow road of the Gods. Freya had learned about it in Sunday school. Bifrost, built by the Immortals, connecting their sky-world to earth.

And now it was no longer night, but day. She was walking up a gently sloping rainbow across a blue sky.

Mum was right, thought Freya. My mum was right. (Oh, how it pained her to even *think* those words.) The Gods exist. They really truly exist.

The immensity of what was happening overwhelmed her.

I can't do this, she thought suddenly. Her parents had always warned her, don't go anywhere with strangers. And yet she'd been swept off by the strangest strangers in the world.

She turned and started re-tracing her steps downwards, trying to ignore the sickening way Bifrost swayed.

'Hey! Where are you going?' shouted the boy-king.

She ignored him and started to run. The boy blocked her in a flash. One moment he was behind her, the next in front.

'You can't go back.'

'I can! I will!' said Freya.

'Look down,' said the boy.

Freya glanced down for a moment, then wished she hadn't. She was bad with heights. She suddenly remembered the terrible moment she'd been travelling in the lift high up the Eiffel Tower, when she started shaking and sweating as the ground receded beneath her. Her stomach lurched as she glimpsed flame-bright water below. Water that looked nothing like the turgid Thames.

She wanted to clutch onto the side but the red flames stopped her. Her knees wobbled. Then her stomach lurched again, and she vomited.

The boy-king caught her arm.

'Don't worry, you'll get used to the wobbling. Bifrost is strange the first few times, then you don't even notice it shakes.'

Freya's mouth tasted sour. She panted and wiped her lips on her frayed sweatshirt sleeve.

'Come on,' said the boy. 'We don't have much time.'

Freya allowed him to lead her.

'I don't understand,' said Freya. 'Where did Bifrost come from? I've been on the Millennium Bridge before and I've never seen it.'

The boy-king smiled.

'Only people the Gods wish to see can cross over to their world.'

Then the boy suddenly dashed ahead and started turning cartwheels like a mad imp. His crown rolled off and slid down the curving rainbow road.

'Oh Gods, how wonderful to feel my body again. Hello, legs! Hello, arms! Hello, toes!' He hugged himself tightly then did a little dance.

'Roskva! Isn't it wonderful to stretch your legs again!' he yelled to the silent queen walking ahead of him, leading the huge grey stallion as easily as if he were a greyhound.

'Who are you?' said Freya.

'I'm Thialfi. Alfi,' he said, swooping down and replacing the crown on his head in one graceful move. 'That's my sister, Roskva. Grump-face we called her at home.'

Roskva turned and stuck out her tongue at him.

'But *who* are you?' said Freya.

'Who are *you*?' said Roskva. 'You're very pale. Do you sleep in a grave mound with corpses?'

'No!' said Freya. What a mean cow Roskva was. 'I'm Freya.'

Roskva looked astonished. 'I've lived in Asgard and I know the goddess Freyja. She's extremely beautiful. You most certainly aren't her.'

'I never said I was,' said Freya. 'I'm just named after her.'

Freya stared at Roskva. Roskva held her gaze. Her lip curled faintly.

I don't believe kings and queens are any better than anyone else and I won't be scared of her, thought Freya.

'Why can you speak English?' she said.

Alfi snorted.

'Where are the toilets?'

'I'm sorry?' said Freya.

'Où sont les toilettes? ¿dónde están los aseos? Dov'è la toilette? Waar is het toilet? ГДЕ ТУАЛЕТЫ?' said Alfi. 'We've been frozen in that place of dead things for years and years and years.' He shivered. 'Listening and waiting . . . All those people . . . Babble babble babble. Where were we?'

Freya swallowed. 'London. The British Museum.'

Alfi shrugged. 'Before that it seems we were in a sand dune on an island called Lewis. Do you know it?'

Freya shook her head. Her throat was parched.

Roskva said nothing. Tears dripped down her face.

'I hate you, Alfi. I hate you.'

'Can't you stop?' said Alfi. 'Can't you let it go?'

Roskva shook her head. She patted the grey horse's muzzle and murmured to him. The horse snorted.

'We are the playthings of the Gods,' said Roskva. Her feet stomped as she walked.

But I'm not, thought Freya. 'Why am *I* here? I have a history test tomorrow on Tudor England. I haven't written my book report . . .'

'You called us,' said Alfi. 'You blew Heimdall's horn.'

'I didn't mean to! I think there's been a terrible mistake.'

'You called us. You woke us. It is your fate. That cannot be changed.'

'No,' said Freya. 'That can't be my fate.'

'Fate is stronger and the Gods mightier than anyone can imagine,' said Roskva. 'When the Gods give orders, we obey. My life has never gone according to *my* wishes.' She looked at Freya curiously. 'What strange clothes you wear. No cloak. No arm rings. No jewellery at all.'

'We're not allowed to wear jewellery in school,' said Freya.

'School?' said Alfi.

26

'Where you learn stuff,' said Freya.

Alfi frowned. Then his face cleared.

'Of course,' said Alfi. He looked at her respectfully. 'Of course. You must have great wisdom for the fates to have chosen you.'

Freya didn't like the sound of that.

'Chosen me for *what?*' said Freya.

Roskva snorted unpleasantly. 'Ha.'

'The All-Father of Asgard, who rules all things, will explain,' said Alfi.

Freya's eyes widened.

'You mean . . . Woden?'

Alfi looked at her and smiled.

'Woden. Odin. All-Father. The Much-Wise. The God of Victory. The One-eyed. Who else?'

Freya shook her head. 'He's going to . . . *talk* to me?'

She was having trouble breathing. The Gods didn't meet humans. Long, long ago they did, but not now.

They fell silent. There was just the sound of their feet, padding on the bridge, and the huge grey horse skittering and snorting and jerking his head as he meekly followed Roskva, unperturbed by the flames leaping around him. Freya felt hot and a little out of breath. She took off her sweatshirt and tied it round her waist. She still couldn't see the end of the rainbow bridge, lost in the clouds and mist above them.

Alfi raced ahead, a blur of speed, then just as quickly dashed back. His fingers drummed restlessly against his sides as he fell into step beside Freya. Roskva walked on her other side, the stallion following obediently behind them. Just in case I make a run for it, thought Freya.

'Has the dark season started yet?' said Alfi.

'Dark season?' said Freya. 'It's spring. And the year is 5012 AW.'

Alfi looked bewildered.

'What do those numbers mean?'

How can he not know this? thought Freya. 'According to the sacred Edda, Woden and his brothers created the world 5012 years ago,' she recited. 'AW means the years after Woden's birth. So A = after, W = Woden. Of course the earth is much older than that, but—'

Freya broke off. Somehow it seemed rude to question when the world began in front of the deities who for all she knew had been there when Woden used the eyebrows of the frost giant Ymir to make the earth and his blood to form the lakes and the oceans.

'You *are* gods, right?' Freya asked cautiously.

'We're human,' said Roskva. 'Like you.'

Freya gasped.

'But you've walked with the Gods,' said Freya. 'You've lived with them.'

'Humph,' said Roskva. 'If you like that sort of thing.'

'Don't listen to her,' said Alfi. 'We know how much thanks we owe to fate. You can never tell what will bring you luck.'

Freya stared at them in awe. They must be the luckiest humans who ever lived.

'If you're not a goddess, Roskva, then what are you queen of?' asked Freya.

'Queen?'

'Your crown,' said Freya, pointing.

'Oh that. Ha.' Roskva laughed. 'I'm queen of nothing. Not even myself. I'm Thor's bondservant. Thanks to my greedy-pig brother there. This is all your fault, Alfi!'

Freya was startled by the venom in her voice.

'Oh Gods, Roskva, when will you let it alone?' said Alfi. He clenched his fists and drummed them against his legs.

So Roskva was Thor's slave. Oh. Freya flushed, and not just from the heat of the rainbow's flames.

'Alfi? Are you a king?' she asked.

'If only,' said Alfi. 'I'm also Thor's bondservant.'

How awful to be a slave, even if your master was a God. Freya wished she hadn't asked.

'Our life was stolen long ago,' said Roskva, as if she could read Freya's thoughts.

'What do you mean?' said Freya. 'How old *are* you?'

Roskva scrunched up her face. 'Who knows? I don't remember any more. We were children when Thor took us from our parents. Now . . . we're still children. Just old ones.'

'Why did he take you?' asked Freya. Once she started asking questions, she always found it hard to stop.

'It's a long story,' said Alfi.

Suddenly Freya had a horrible thought.

'Am I going to be a slave too?' said Freya.

Alfi laughed and shook his head.

'Then why are we going to Asgard? You must tell me.'

'Because we've been summoned,' said Alfi.

'But why?' said Freya. 'What happens if we *don't* go?'

Roskva and Alfi glanced at each other. The great horse shook his head and flicked his ears nervously.

Alfi shrugged. 'We have no choice.'

'I know you're slaves, but why don't you just run away?' persisted Freya.

Roskva slapped her. Freya stepped backwards,

clutching her stinging cheek. She wanted to slap her right back but something about Roskva's stony face stopped her.

'When Gods give orders we obey,' said Roskva.

'And even if we *could* run, where would we go?' said Alfi. 'Our parents have been dead for thousands of years. We have nowhere to go but Asgard.'

But I do, thought Freya.

'You know I can't stay for long,' said Freya. 'My dad will be worried about me and I'll need to get back.'

Alfi and Roskva looked at each other again.

'What?' said Freya. She began to feel afraid. 'What aren't you telling me?'

There was a clomp-clomp stomp-stomp-stomping behind them. The horse shied.

'Whoa, whoa, Sleipnir,' said Roskva as the huge Bear-Shirt appeared, panting and sweaty. His sword was bloody. Great white gobs of foamy sweat dripped off him as if he were an animal. He looked as grey and dirty as a block of broken ice.

'We thought we'd lost you,' said Alfi.

I wish we had, thought Freya, shrinking back.

The giant man grunted. He wiped his iron-studded sword on his skins, leaving a reddish streak across his huge chest. Freya trembled. His fist was like a club.

His bulging arms were thicker than a man's thighs. His crooked, bristly grey eyebrows met in the middle and his face was criss-crossed with scars.

His black raven shield, which he carried slung over his arm, was overlaid with gold and embossed with jewels.

'What's your name?' asked Roskva.

The berserk grunted again.

'Snot.'

'Snot? But that's a girl's name,' said Roskva.

'It's not,' he growled. The knotted muscles on his neck bulged.

'I'm sure it is,' Roskva said. 'The next farm over had a girl called Snot. Remember, Alfi? Ugly little troll she was, too, with all those cracked teeth. Snot? Really? Did your parents want a girl or something?'

'Say that again and I'll kill you,' said Snot.

Roskva opened her mouth, then closed it. Holding tight to Sleipnir's bridle, she stomped on ahead.

'I remember you,' said Alfi. 'You arrived at Valhalla, ignored the place Woden assigned you and yanked two men out of their seats and took their places.'

'And you were the one we threw bones at,' said Snot.

Alfi looked away. A faint blush spread over his face and neck.

Freya didn't know what to say. She was usually the picked-on one, too.

'Come on,' shouted Roskva. 'We're almost there! If we're lucky, Heimdall will have cake and mead to welcome us home. He'll have seen us coming ages ago.'

Freya forgot how tired she felt and how much her legs ached.

Asgard! The great fortress of the Gods. The lush green meadows, the palace roofs thatched with gleaming gold. The sky-high stone ramparts built by a giant, protecting the mighty palaces of shining silver. Asgard.

Oh, Mum, if you could see me now, thought Freya, as she stepped off the trembling rainbow into the realm of the Gods.

3 The Well of Urd

'Yoo-hoo! Hello! It's us! Roskva and Alfi. Hello!'

'Who are you calling?' asked Freya, gaping at the curving wall of golden-brown rocks and boulders that soared upward into the bright sky, high as a mountain, higher than any wall she'd ever seen. She felt tiny and insignificant standing beneath the gigantic ramparts.

'Heimdall,' said Roskva. 'Hellooooo! Heimdall!'

The guardian of the Gods, the one whose horn she'd blown. He'd be angry with her for her terrible presumption, she thought, shrinking inside.

'He lives at the end of heaven outside the wall . . .

guarding the bridge,' muttered Alfi. 'Where could he be?'

Roskva looked around. 'He never leaves the heaven-mountain,' she said.

'Maybe he didn't hear you,' said Freya.

'The Wind-Shield of the Gods can hear the grass growing on earth,' said Alfi. 'He can hear the wool growing on sheep. He can hear fish breathing in the sea.'

'He heard us,' said Roskva. She looked grim.

'But where's Heimdall's palace?' said Alfi. 'It should be over there.' He pointed to a barren stretch of land, with weeds growing amidst piles of stones and rubble. 'There, under the wall, at the end of the bridge.'

Freya stared at the ruin. Roskva and Alfi exchanged rapid words in their own language.

'What are you saying?' said Freya. She heard the fear in their voices.

They ignored her.

'Maybe he moved,' said Freya.

'Maybe the All-Father gave him a better palace,' said Alfi.

'It's possible,' said Roskva. She looked doubtful.

'Roskva, I'm scared,' said Alfi.

'Let's go in,' said Roskva quietly. 'There's the little

36

doorway we can creep through.'

'It'll be locked,' said Alfi.

'Then we'll just have to break it, won't we?' said Roskva. 'We don't have time to wait for Heimdall to get back from wherever he is.'

Sleipnir suddenly reared and snorted and dug his hooves into the ground. However hard Roskva and Alfi tugged on his bridle, he wouldn't budge.

'Leave him,' said Snot. He gnawed on his shield and bared his chipped black teeth. His matted grey wolf-hair stood up in bristly tufts. His rank smell was unbearable. Freya turned her face away from him, but Roskva and Alfi didn't seem to notice.

They left Sleipnir beside the flaming bridge, and stood before the wooden door, studded with nails and criss-crossed with iron bars, cut into a gigantic doorway. Roskva tugged hard on the rusty latch, which fell off in her hand. She bit her lip, and pushed the door open. With a screech, the door splintered and snapped off its great hinges.

'Get your sword out, you stinking son of a mare!' snapped Snot. 'Never walk ahead of your weapon.'

Alfi blushed and drew his sword.

Then, one by one, they walked through the gateway into Asgard.

Freya gasped. For once, she couldn't speak as she looked around the stronghold of the Gods.

Tumbleweed blew across the desolate plains. Thistles and brambles covered the parched ground. There were no shimmering green and gold fields rolling out to infinity. No mighty gleaming citadels. Just nettles growing higher than any Freya had ever seen.

Where were the palaces? All she could see was the wind-swept world tree Yggdrasil soaring high into the heavens. She heard the far-off roar of torrential rivers. Otherwise all was silent, as if Asgard was asleep.

'Are you sure . . . are you sure we're in the right place?' Freya felt overwhelmed with disappointment. Was this some kind of practical joke her weird companions were playing on her? Had they yanked her from her life and dragged her here to roam around a dusty wasteland? How could she have been so gullible to think she'd be meeting the Gods?

She glared at Roskva and Alfi.

Alfi looked ashen. He clutched Roskva's sleeve.

'Do you think the frost giants attacked while we were asleep?' he murmured. 'Could Ragnarok have happened?'

Roskva shook her head. 'The earth still exists. So

does the sun and the moon. We saw the stars tonight. It's not the end of days.'

Snot growled and gripped his sword.

'Who did this? I'll kill them!' he howled. Then, bellowing, 'Valhalla! Valhalla!' he ran towards the remains of a vast, derelict Hall beside a fast-flowing river.

Freya, Alfi, and Roskva followed him. They stood inside the ruined walls, unable to speak. Bits of tarnished metal, scrapings from the vanished roof, and a few rusted spears lay scattered in the dirt.

This was Valhalla. The Hall of the Slain. The gold-bright palace of Woden's chosen warriors. The dark, echoing wine hall was now only home to the winds.

'This hall was so bright they used swords instead of fire for light,' murmured Alfi. 'The rafters were made of spear shafts and thatched with overlapping shields of gold. There were helmets and red-gold mail coats strewn everywhere, and men shouting and drinking . . . even Woden's wolves are gone; I used to give them meat scraps . . . there were five hundred and forty doors. I know, I used to walk around and count them while the Valkyries, the Choosers of the Slain, served mead and haunches of boar to the tired warriors. That's the corner where I tried to barricade myself from the men who pelted me with bones when they'd finished eating and my Master wasn't there to protect me.'

Freya's skin prickled. She was reminded of old photographs of American ghost towns, where only a few sun-bleached buildings and dirt roads showed that anyone had ever lived there. She felt as if she were walking in an ancient graveyard, untouched and unvisited for centuries, with tumbled-down stones and worn-out inscriptions the only signs of the people who had once walked the earth.

Snot stared at the shards of a black cauldron in the middle of the floor, and kicked at a few shield fragments. A rotten, sagging mead-bench was shoved against what was left of a wall. He picked it up and hurled it against the ground where it splintered. 'I sat here,' he muttered. 'Woden put me in a low place by a door, because I was newly arrived and yet to prove myself. Ha! I didn't stay there long. As they say, fast temper grows in a seat far from the High Table.' He sighed. 'We fought all day and feasted all night.'

'Didn't that get boring?' blurted Freya, before she could stop herself.

Snot glowered down at her over his raven shield. His dark eyes glinted beneath his crooked brows.

'How else can you forget your self?' he said.

Freya wished she'd kept her mouth shut. Snot frightened her and she wanted to keep away from him as much as possible. She left him to his memories inside the ruins of Valhalla and walked over to where Alfi and Roskva were standing amidst dried-out rushes and sedges, watching the river roaring past as if they had lost the will to move.

'The All-Father's palace should be over there,' said Alfi, pointing into empty space. Freya squinted. She could just make out a few piles of stones and pillars far off in the distance. It looked like the ruins of the Roman Forum.

'Let me just have a quick look around,' said Alfi. 'Wait here.'

Freya watched astonished, as he ran off. One moment he was there, the next . . . not.

'He's fast,' said Freya.

'They say only thought can outrun him,' said Roskva. 'Bit of an exaggeration, but he's pretty speedy.'

There was a flash of movement, and Alfi had returned.

'Njord's palace, and Freyja's, and Sif's . . . none of them exist any more,' said Alfi, panting. 'It's all just rubble and ruins.'

'Where is everyone?' said Freya.

They ignored her.

'Master! Master!' shouted Roskva. 'Master! Are you here?'

There was a rusty upturned chariot, half-buried in the dirt, choked with weeds. A twisted rope of silver tarnished black lay beside it.

Roskva prodded her brother.

'That's our Master's!' she hissed.

'No,' said Alfi. 'It can't be . . .' He picked up the silver reins and scraped at the tarnish, revealing traces of the interwoven pattern. Then he nodded.

'Roskva, what are we going to do? Do you think we're too late?'

Roskva twisted her hands. Freya noticed how old and wrinkled and calloused they were. More like the hands of an old woman than a girl. Her nails were bitten.

'Could the Gods be – *dead*?' Alfi whispered the last word as if terrified he would be overheard.

Roskva laughed. 'The Gods are immortal.'

'Something's happened,' said Alfi.

'We've seen no burial mounds,' said Roskva.

'Maybe there was a fire . . . maybe the Gods have gone somewhere else . . .'

'But that doesn't explain . . . all this,' said Roskva.

'This is so much worse . . . How much time has passed since we were here?'

Alfi shrugged. 'How can I answer that?'

'I know things were bad, but . . .' Roskva trailed off.

'If no one's here then I'll be going home,' said Freya. She felt angry and frightened.

'You're going nowhere, hornblower,' said Roskva.

'Since when are you my boss?' said Freya.

Roskva waved her hands as if she were brushing off an ant.

'You know nothing, little girl!' hissed Roskva. 'You are part of something much bigger than you can imagine.'

Little girl? Freya opened her mouth to protest.

'We'll argue about this later,' said Roskva. 'Let's go to the Well. If any of the Immortals are still here, that's where they'll be.'

'The Gods hold court at the Well of Urd under Yggdrasil every day to pass judgement,' Alfi told Freya as they walked through the weeds towards the tallest, widest, most enormous tree she'd ever seen or imagined. Dead ivy coiled round its withered trunk. The towering tree hurtled into the heavens higher than she could see, wider than a street of houses, wider than Buckingham Palace. Its leafless branches fanned out across the sky.

'Roskva and I came here every day with our Master. He lived so far away in Asgard we had to wade across many rivers to get here. But we did it. The Master was always moving, always travelling, always fighting and bellowing. It was hard to keep up with him.'

They walked to the sacred Well of Fate beneath one of the roots of the world tree. Reverently, Freya brushed her hand along the rough bark of the great ash, which loomed above the holy place of the Gods. Her fingers tingled as she felt the tree's faint pulse.

Freya stood in the middle of a circle of intricately carved, ivory-white stones, their seats worn smooth. Tracery lines of runes were etched along the bottom. Moss and grasses grew around them. At the centre was a large pool with glinting blue-black water, nestling under the root of the giant ash tree. A single shaft of sunlight lit up the well.

There was a hushed silence. Freya felt the power of the place.

'That's where the great god Frey sat,' said Alfi, pointing to the stone seat still decorated with the outline of a giant boar. 'And that's the All-Father's High Seat. His wife Frigg sat beside him. Baldr the Fair and Heimdall over there. And the beautiful goddess Freyja, Frey's sister, across from Woden and his wife. Our Master Thor and his wife Sif sat here. Roskva and I stood behind him in case he needed us.'

Freya walked to the pool and knelt down to peer into the inky depths. She picked up a small stone and was about to drop it in when Roskva gasped and stopped her.

'That's a sacred well,' she said. 'The Well of Fate. You don't just throw things in it.'

'Oh,' said Freya. She stepped back as if the well had caught fire. 'I just wanted to see how deep it was.'

'She didn't mean any harm,' said Alfi. 'Remember when all this was new to you too, Roskva.'

Roskva scowled. Freya thought for a wild moment how nice it would be to dump Roskva down the well.

Roskva scooped up a handful of water and sprinkled it on the bark of the giant tree. Yggdrasil shuddered and jolted, and a burst of dark green leaves appeared on the lower branches.

'Well? What do we do now?' said Freya.

'About bloody time,' hissed a voice beside her.

'What took you so long?' rasped another.

Freya jumped. She looked around, but saw nothing. Roskva tensed.

'We've been waiting centuries for you,' moaned a peevish voice behind her.

The shadows fluttered. Freya saw ghosts rise from the earth and the rocks and shuffle towards her, tottering creatures of twilight and dew, more like walking air than living beings. Freya could hear bones creaking, like rusty wheels trying to turn again. She smelled mould and damp, as if the lid of an old trunk filled with moth-eaten rags had suddenly been lifted.

Roskva gasped. She clutched Alfi's arm. Snot growled.

Alfi nudged her. 'That's Heimdall,' he murmured, pointing to a wizened spectre babbling to himself as he rocked back and forth. 'Oh Thor, that's the guardian of the Gods. Roskva. Look at him. He's worse than Grandpa was . . .'

The wispy, flickering shadows gathered in the stone circle under Yggdrasil's withered root. The dying Gods were assembling to hold their court.

A crippled, shrivelled wraith hunched on the highest stone seat. His single eye glittered faintly beneath a few threads hanging down from what was once a wide-brimmed hat. Fragments of a blue mantle clung to the bones jutting out from his emaciated body.

Snot fell to the ground.

'Bow!' hissed Roskva, flinging herself down. Alfi

did the same. Freya copied. She tried to stop her hands shaking.

'Who is that old guy?' she whispered.

'The All-Father,' murmured Alfi. 'Hide your eyes.' Freya obeyed. Her heart was pounding.

It was impossible. How could this doddery, broken-backed wreck be Woden the Much-Wise, Father of Magic, Giver of Victory, Lord of Poetry? Freya glimpsed the stone seat beneath his transparent skin. The capricious, scary, vengeful God, the one Clare bowed down to so anxiously, was a crumpled husk. Two dead ravens, skeletons with a few feathers sticking out from their sides, perched on his shoulders.

'Stand up!' croaked the one-eyed ghost. 'Our time is brief.'

The four stood in the middle of the stone circle, surrounded by the trembling Gods. Freya felt faint with horror and pity. The immortal Gods were old and dying. How was this possible?

'Where is the hero we've been waiting for?' rasped Woden. 'Where is the battle-brave warrior who blew Heimdall's horn and woke my sleeping army? Where is the mortal hero the seeress foretold? Let him step forward and reveal himself.'

He can't mean me, thought Freya. She looked

down at her scuffed black shoes and her Baldr's Fane of England school uniform with its crumpled blue-pleated skirt. There was still a ketchup stain from lunch on her ratty yellow sweatshirt. *He can't mean me.*

Freya looked around. Snot scratched his bum. Alfi cleared his throat. Roskva gave her a push.

'Who blew the horn and cracked open the earth? Step forward!' hissed Woden. His withered eye flashed for a moment.

'I did,' whispered Freya.

The assembled Gods hissed and muttered. The Goddess Sif choked. Heimdall rocked to and fro, drooling.

'But it was a mistake,' said Freya. 'I didn't mean to . . . I didn't know, I . . .'

'Your name,' said Woden. When he spoke, there was an edge to his voice that frightened her.

'Freya,' she said.

'An unworthy namesake,' hissed a bald Goddess with shaking, liver-coloured hands. Her transparent skin was a mass of wrinkles. A glittering gold necklace weighed down her scrawny, turkey-gobbler neck. 'You're so ugly. What were your parents thinking? I am insulted.'

You're one to talk, you old crone, thought Freya. And she'd always been so proud to share the name of such a beautiful, wise Immortal.

Woden fixed the Goddess Freyja with his dark, baleful eye. She tossed her wobbly head as if she still had flaxen curls to toss. Her necklace rattled.

'Your parents' names?' said Woden.

'Bob . . . uh . . . Robert Gislason,' said Freya. 'My mother is Clare Raven.'

'You and your family are unknown to me,' said Woden. He sat for a long moment in silence. 'There was a time when no creature on earth escaped my notice.'

'I am Frey,' quavered a stooping God with tightly stretched, blackened skin. He looked like rags fluttering on a stick. 'Are you a thrall?'

'A thrall?'

'A slave,' said Frey.

'No!' said Freya.

'A farmer then?' asked the God of crops and sunshine and peace and plenty.

'No,' said Freya.

'Surely not a noble?'

'No,' said Freya. How her granddad the baker would have loved that question.

'There is nothing else,' said Frey.

The Gods and Goddesses jittered and stuttered.

'Not a slave? Then who does the work?'

'We all do,' said Freya.

'We've been dying too long,' whispered Sif, a heap of shrivelled, transparent skin, her wispy white hairs barely covering her bald skull. 'We'll have a lot to learn . . .'

'A lot to put right,' quavered Woden's wife, Frigg. Her toothless mouth sagged.

'Can I go home now?' said Freya.

'Hold your tongue,' ordered Woden. Freya shrank back.

'What was I saying?' muttered Woden. He was silent for a long moment, mumbling to himself. 'Oh yes,' he rasped. 'Where are the others? Where are my sword-bright warriors? Where are the ones versed in the arts of old magic? Where is the sleeping army who will save us?'

Freya looked around. Alfi, Roskva, and Snot did the same. She half-expected to see all the chess pieces gathering, the knights, the kings, the queens, the pawns, all changed back into living people, but there were only the empty plains of Asgard and the wrecked, racked Gods shaking before her.

'It's just . . . us, Lord,' said Roskva. 'We're the only ones who woke when she blew the horn.'

The assembled Gods murmured.

'*This* is our sleeping army! Four? Just . . . *four*? These . . . mortals! These . . . these – children!' spat a toothless God.

'I'm no child,' said Snot. The gnarled skin on his thick neck tensed. 'I'm not a babysitter either. I was one of Woden's berserks.'

'Alfi and I can take care of ourselves,' said Roskva.

I can't, Freya wanted to whimper.

'The charm is weakening,' whispered Woden. 'The whole army should have woken . . . There should be over a hundred warriors here . . . My powers are fading.'

The assembled Gods sighed. The Goddess Freyja began to weep. Tears of gold fell from the cataract-covered eyes and plinked on the dirt. Someone Freya presumed was the Goddess's husband leaned over to wipe her eyes, but she pushed him away.

'We are nothing more now than breath in the trees, the rustling of leaves, the foam on the waves. We who used to make and destroy, reduced to rustling,' moaned Sif.

'I HATE rustling,' hissed the Goddess Freyja. Her palsied hands shook.

'Wait . . . for . . . me!' gasped a voice.

'Master?' breathed Alfi. His eyes filled with tears as he bowed to the frail, dripping-wet man with a hint of a red beard still visible on his gaunt jaw. He paused to regain his breath at every painful step.

Freya stared. This was Thor? The mighty Thor, the killer of giants? The God who could devour an ox and eight salmon at one sitting, who heaved boulders and shattered cliffs? The God of thunder and stormy skies?

Roskva looked shocked. 'Master.' Almost unwillingly she smiled. 'Still wading through all those rivers to get here, I see.'

'Ah, Roskva. Thialfi.' A tiny smile flittered across the skull-like face. 'You've returned to save us. At last.'

'As if we had any—' began Roskva.

'Of course we have,' interrupted Alfi, kicking her.

Roskva kicked him back.

'Ow,' said Alfi. 'That hurt.'

'Good,' said Roskva.

'Good to see you, my boy, good to see you both,' gasped Thor. ''Course I can't see you, too blind now, but I heard your voices. You are still young. That's good. That's very good. Speak again.'

'Master,' said Alfi, brushing tears away from his eyes, 'where's your hammer?'

'Hammer?' muttered Thor. 'What hammer?'

Roskva gasped. 'Your hammer, Mjollnir. The one you use to smash giants. The one only you can lift. Mjollnir.'

'Ah!' said Thor. 'I knew I'd forgotten something. Mjollnir . . . yes, now where did I put it?' He looked around as if the hammer would appear before him.

Snot grunted and said nothing.

'Tell me one thing,' rasped Woden. 'Are we still worshipped and feared? My ravens who brought me news of the world of men are long dead.'

Freya gulped. What should she say? Dare she tell him about the half-empty fanes attended mainly by old ladies or students praying for extra wisdom during exams? Oh and of course by families trying to get their children into the local Fane of England school who turned up every Sunday for a few years till priests like her mum wrote a letter to the headteacher testifying to their attendance and then . . . poof! Never seen again until they wanted a fane wedding or a baby-naming?

And what about all the other religions?

'Answer me,' ordered Woden.

'Lots of people worship and honour you,' said Freya. 'Your High Priests sit in the House of Lords. The Queen of England is the head of your Fane.'

Woden groaned. The assembled Gods groaned with him. The air filled with sighs.

'Just lots? *Lots!* Not all? It's as I feared — there are other gods now . . . taking our place,' hissed Woden. 'False gods. And we can do nothing to destroy them while we are . . . like this.'

'Why do people worship other gods besides us?' said Njord, God of winds and wealth. '*We* are the Immortals! We gave them sun, and crops, and fish in the sea and oxen to till the land, and battles to fight, and Valhalla for the brave . . .'

'Our gifts to mankind are poorly repaid,' said Frey. 'We demand to be worshipped. We are the Lords your Gods. You shall have no other gods before us.'

'Lots of worshippers is still good,' said Freya.

'You're lying,' said Frigg.

'I no longer smell sacrifices,' said Woden.

Freya didn't know what to say. How could Woden not know that sacrifices stopped hundreds of years ago?

'My mother is your priestess. She has a big throng every Sunday at her fane,' said Freya. 'And on feast days it's packed.'

Woden looked as if he could see straight into her thoughts.

'You're lying. Again.'

'I'm not lying,' said Freya. 'I'm . . . umm . . .' She was saying what she thought he wanted to hear.

'You were saying what you thought I wanted to hear,' said Woden. 'I crave knowledge, not lies.'

Freya bowed her head.

'I always got more sacrifices than you,' said Njord.

'Didn't,' said one-handed Tyr.

'Did!'

'I had more temples than all of you,' said Thor.

'I want my gold-bright hall again,' whispered Frigg.

'I want my beauty,' moaned the Goddess Freyja.

'I want to kill giants,' said Thor.

'Eh?' said Heimdall, waking up. 'Giants? Where?'

'What's happened to you, Lords?' said Freya. She felt bewildered. 'Why am I here?'

Woden smiled a ghost of a smile.

'The hornblower brings us back to our business,' he said. 'Listen carefully. Our time is very short.'

Freya strained to hear his faint voice. Roskva stifled a yawn. Alfi jabbed her in the ribs. She glared at him.

Woden cleared his throat. 'The Goddess Idunn, who guarded the apples of immortality which we ate to keep us young, was stolen from us by the giant Thjazi. Loki the Trickster—' the Gods moaned and snarled at Loki's name, drowning out Woden's feeble

55

voice. He raised his skeletal hand to quiet them.

'Loki gave her to that evil giant, may curses rain upon him and fire consume him and his hearth. We ordered Loki to bring Idunn back. But he – and she – never returned.'

Freya gasped.

'Idunn never came back?'

'No,' said Woden.

'But everyone knows that Loki rescued Idunn,' she said. 'The Gods regained their youth. Loki returned to Asgard with Idunn and her apples . . . it says so in the sacred Edda . . .'

Woden glared at her with his dark, deadly eye. Freya shrank back. Snot scowled.

'That was the story we told. You think we wanted the world to know the truth? Loki never came back. Whether because he wouldn't, or because he couldn't, even I don't know. Loki is the son of a giant, a trickster, a shape-shifter, and the father of lies. We've been dying from the moment he led Idunn out of Asgard. We who were beyond time are now its subjects. Then the sleeping army . . . the army I . . .'

Woden trailed off. Drool dribbled from his mouth and down his chin. Freya averted her eyes. He reminded her, horribly, of her old cat, Caesar, who'd shrunk to a tottery grey ghost before he died.

'I have lost the thread of my thoughts,' murmured Woden. He struck himself hard on the forehead. Some of the Gods, who'd been dozing, startled awake.

'You were telling them about the sleeping army,' hissed Frigg. 'Be quick about it.'

'Ah yes,' said Woden. His voice was getting fainter. Freya moved closer to hear him. She was longing to sit down and rest.

'Sit,' said Woden. 'All of you.'

Alfi, Roskva, and Freya gathered at his feet. Only Snot remained standing.

'Long, long ago, when all was well with Gods and men, I wove a mighty charm and sent an army to sleep under the mountains. There they would lie, my hidden warriors, disguised as chess pieces, ready to wake when Heimdall's horn summoned them. I thought the twilight of the Gods would be far, far off. I did not know a time of deadly peril would arrive so much sooner . . . even I cannot foresee everything.'

Woden sighed. There was a faint snoring sound. The Goddess Freyja kicked her husband to wake him. Sif sat listening, twisting her gnarled hands. The others dozed, their heads sinking to their shrunken, wrinkled chests.

'At first, when Loki did not return, I sent Valhalla's best warriors to find Idunn, but . . . they failed. I sent more heroes, snatched from the world of men. They also failed.

'It was time to wake the sleeping army, but the horn had vanished. Heimdall had hidden it somewhere in a spring to keep it safe, but by now his mind had gone, he could no longer remember where, he kept saying, 'What horn? What horn?'

The Gods sighed and glared at Heimdall.

'What horn?' said Heimdall.

'Oh shut up!' snapped Sif.

'We searched and searched, but we were now too weak to leave Asgard. The horn was never found.

'With the last of my strength I sacrificed my horse, Sleipnir, and the two young mortals amongst us, Roskva and Thialfi, to sleep with the army and guide them here when a great hero found the horn and woke them.

'And so it has come to pass as the seeress foretold. Heimdall's horn was blown at long last.

'But the entire army didn't wake. Just . . . you.'

Roskva and Alfi glanced at one another. Snot gripped his sword and growled under his breath.

Uh-oh, thought Freya. Uh-oh. I don't like the

58

sound of this. Could Woden hear her heart banging against her chest?

'Our fate is a harsh one, Lord,' said Roskva. Alfi poked her.

'Fate rules all our lives,' said Woden. 'Even the Gods.'

'Just tell me who to kill,' said Snot. 'My sword is sharp and ready.'

'You four are our last hope,' said Woden.

'Ha!' snorted Sif.

'Some hope,' muttered Frigg.

Woden ignored them.

'You must save us. The giant Thjazi took Idunn the ever-young to his storm-home high in the mountains of Jotunheim. Go to the realm of the giants. Find Idunn and bring her back. Otherwise, we will die.

'And when we die the weeping world will die with us. The ice is melting. I can feel it. I can hear it. Drip. Drip. Drip. The waters are rising. The Frost Giants will rise up, freed from their icy bonds. Then the Axe-Age and the Wind-Age and the Wolf-Age will be upon the earth.'

Let the ice melt, thought Freya viciously. She felt as if she were struggling through quicksand. What can *I* do? Find Idunn? Find Thjazi? What?

'Don't ask me to do this,' Freya whimpered. She

59

thought of terrible things she'd been forced to do in the past. Wear a hideous pink dress to the school disco. Babysit her bratty cousin. Eat beetroot. Walk to the top of Arthur's Seat in the Edinburgh rain. Invite Grisla Taylor to her birthday party. Sing a solo at Ruth Kirsch's bat-mitzvah. Clean her bedroom *every* Saturday. Go on a rollercoaster.

'You will do as you're told,' said Tyr. 'We are the Lords your Gods.'

Alfi looked at Freya open-mouthed. Then he fell to his knees.

'We are ready to obey,' he said.

'Tell us where to go,' said Roskva.

'I will kill Thjazi, I vow it,' said Snot.

Everything was happening too fast.

'Wait!' said Freya. She jumped to her feet. 'Wait. I'm a schoolgirl. I'm not even old enough to stay home alone at night. Of course if I were, then I wouldn't be here, would I? This is all some terrible mistake. I blew the horn by accident and I was in the stupid museum by accident because my dad is stupid and my parents are divorced. Please. You can't ask me to do this. I don't even have a coat with me!' she wailed.

Roskva muttered under her breath. 'I'd shut up if I were you.'

'It is not for you to decide yes or no,' said the Father of All. 'It's enough that I command it.'

'You can't make me.' Freya felt as if a bratty voice inside her was speaking. Fear made her reckless.

The assembled Gods gasped and hissed. Thor half-rose, but couldn't get up and collapsed back on to the stone.

Roskva muttered under her breath. 'I'd really shut up if I were you. He's killed people for much less.'

'You DARE to challenge the will of the All-Father, Waker of the Dead, Giver of Victory, the All-Mighty, the . . .' Woden broke off, coughing, hacking, wheezing and clutching his wizened chest. 'Don't you want to outlive your mortality?' he rasped. 'Life is so short. You came from darkness and in a few flaps of a raven's wing you will return to darkness. Without renown, without glory, you are nothing. You'll be nothing. You should be eager for fame.' His filmy eye glared at her contemptuously.

Eager for fame? Freya looked bewildered at the one-eyed God as he swayed before her, gasping for breath. Of course she wanted to be famous. Didn't everyone? But she wanted to be a famous rock star. A famous writer. A famous palaeontologist. A famous tap dancer (even though she had two left feet – a girl could dream, couldn't she?). Not a famous – uhh – giant killer. Or a famous apple snatcher.

Right now she'd gladly settle for being alive, a little unfamous nobody.

'I want to go home,' said Freya. 'Please find someone else.'

'You're pathetic,' said Snot. 'My sheep are braver than you.'

'Good for them,' said Freya. 'They can take my place.'

'The length of your life and the day of your death was fated long ago,' whispered Thor. 'So you might as well live fearlessly while you can.'

'My mum – my dad will be worried about me,' said Freya.

Woden shrugged. 'Then you will join the others,' he said softly.

'What others?' said Freya.

'All the other chess pieces,' murmured Woden. 'So many more than a single chess set needs. You remember that multitude of queens? Those extra kings? Those rows and rows of knights and pawns? They're the warriors I sent first, the ones who survived, the ones who failed to find Idunn.'

Freya trembled.

'The chess pieces . . . in the museum?'

'You will become a chess piece and sleep with the army — till another hero rouses them.' Woden fixed her with his crazed eye. 'And since you care so little for renown, I think you will sleep as a pawn.'

Freya could not stop shaking. To be frozen . . . lacking in fate, trapped in a glass case . . . the horror of it overwhelmed her.

I'll run away, she thought frantically. I'll hide and no one will—

'In nine nights your fate will catch up with you wheresoever you are,' said Woden.

'What do you mean?' said Freya. She wished she could stop him reading her thoughts.

'You cannot outrun your fate. Even I cannot change what will be. In nine days and nine nights you will be victorious and live, or fail and turn into ivory.'

Freya closed her eyes. Now she had her bitter answer why the chess pieces looked so glum.

She saw herself on the chessboard, frozen forever, her eyes popping, mouth downturned. What a choice: do nothing and be frozen for ever; do something and fail and be frozen for ever. A wave of dizziness overwhelmed her, and she put her hands on the mossy ground to steady herself.

'Just so I know – what happened to the others?' whispered Freya.

'What others?' said Woden.

'The ones you sent before . . . the ones who didn't return . . .'

'You're wasting time, girl,' hissed Sif.

Woden shrugged. 'Drowned. Killed. Eaten by wolves.'

'Squished by a giant,' said Frey.

'Swept away,' said Thor.

'And one coward jumped off Bifrost,' said Sif.

'Always good to know what I have to look forward to,' said Freya.

Woden almost smiled. 'A death jest. Good.'

I wasn't jesting, thought Freya.

'Go to the realm of the giants. Find Idunn and bring her back. The giant Thjazi took Idunn to Thrymheim, his mountain home. I warn you – he is the most powerful of all the giants.'

'I'm not afraid of giants,' said Snot. 'Though one of Woden's chosen warriors merits worthier companions than two slaves and a . . . not sure what that herring-faced one is,' he added, pointing his thumb at Freya.

Freya whimpered to herself.

'You have nine nights before the charm ends and this

64

brief life will be over for you,' said Woden, struggling to stay awake. 'If you succeed and bring Idunn back to Asgard, your life will be restored to you. If you fail, then you will sleep with the army until the horn is blown again . . . *if* the horn is blown again.'

Freya wanted to cry. And scream. And blame her horrible, stupid squabbling parents. She felt sick to her stomach. If only she could turn back time.

'You cannot struggle against fate,' said Woden.

'We'll leave immediately,' said Alfi.

'With or without this blubbing coward,' said Snot, jerking his head in Freya's direction.

'Coward or no, she must go with,' said Woden. 'That much I know. She blew Heimdall's horn and woke you. Without her, you will fail.'

I think they'll fail with me, thought Freya.

There was a rustling sound as the Gods stirred. Alfi took off his crown and placed it on the ground. After a moment, reluctantly, Roskva did the same.

Is that it? thought Freya frantically.

'Before you go,' said Woden, 'I have secret wisdom, secret runes, the ones I sacrificed my eye for . . .' His hoarse voice trailed off.

'Get on with it, Dad,' rasped Thor. 'They need to go!'

'I can put the sea to sleep,' muttered Woden. 'I can make iron shackles spring open. I can fill foes with panic and weave love charms. I can knock witches off roofs. I can blunt sword blades. I can wake the dead.

'To each of you I will share one rune,' said Woden. 'I have never shared these secrets, torn from the dead, with anyone. What you alone know is most powerful. You will keep these words hidden even from one another. One may know your secret, never a second.'

Woden whispered to Roskva. His claw-like hand gripped her arm. She winced, and nodded. Then he whispered to Alfi. Alfi nodded, and his lips moved, memorising the rune. To Snot he did the same. Snot looked uneasy.

'I'll never remember that!' he burst out.

'Write it down,' said Freya.

'Write?' said Snot. 'No one can write.'

Woden sighed. 'I grow weary,' he whispered. 'Let me teach you your rune, then I must sleep.'

Freya went up to him. He smelled of cold ash and mildew. Reluctantly, she bent closer. Woden whispered in her ear: 'To make a corpse talk, you say: AERKRIUFLT AERKRIUFLT KRIURITHON . . . umm, KRIURTHON . . . or is it THKIRTHU?' Woden broke off and looked away in the distance. 'Well, I'm sure you won't need that one.

Corpses can only tell you so much and their news is usually out of date.'

Freya thought she'd prefer a rune to keep a corpse safely in its mound.

Woden trembled as he gazed at her. 'I must give you something . . . you must have a gift from me . . . lend her your falcon skin,' Woden ordered his wife.

The shrivelled Goddess scowled. Then Frigg reached into her girdle and took out a glowing heap of feathers.

'You'd better bring it back,' she hissed.

'This will turn you into a falcon. With it you can fly anywhere in the nine worlds,' said Woden.

Freya looked at the translucent falcon skin. Fly? Not if she could help it. She was scared of heights. Gingerly, Freya gathered up the feathery skin. It shrank in her hand to a single feather. She shook it out, and it became again a plumed falcon skin. Freya smiled a tiny smile and tucked the feather in her skirt pocket.

'What a shame you don't have Sleipnir. No horse can keep up with him.'

'But we do,' said Roskva. 'He's grazing by Bifrost.'

Woden shook his head.

'My memory,' he muttered. 'My memory. The fates are kind. I wondered where he'd got to . . .

'You have Sleipnir. Good. He can gallop across any

land or up or down any mountain, no matter how steep. No gleaming river or torrential stream can stop him.

'Now swear a ring-oath that you will complete your task, whatever fate may throw in your path,' said Woden.

The God held out his wasted hand. Freya watched as Snot, Alfi, and Roskva placed their hands on top of his ring. Then slowly, reluctantly, she added hers to the pile.

'Swear by the rivers that run through the Underworld,' said Woden. 'Terrible fate-bonds attach to the oath-tearer.' His one eye seared her.

Freya felt icy chills as Woden intoned the fateful words. 'Wretched is the pledge criminal.'

'Wretched is the pledge criminal,' they repeated.

'May Woden hallow this pledge.'

'May Woden hallow this pledge.'

'May Thor hallow these runes.'

'May Thor hallow these runes.'

'So help me Frey and Njord and the all-powerful Gods.'

'So help me Frey and Njord and the all-powerful Gods,' they swore.

'Will the fates favour us?' asked Roskva.

'The seeress said nothing of the future, and it is hidden from me,' said Woden. 'You – berserk. Protect them as you would me.'

68

Snot grunted and bit his shield. He glared at them.

'Always stick together,' whispered Woden. 'You will be stronger that way. Go now. Go swiftly.'

Then the grieving Gods drifted off and faded into the shadows. The stone circle was empty. The only sound was a faint rustling of Yggdrasil's sparse leaves above them.

Freya was alone with Roskva, Alfi, and Snot. She looked around desperately. Maybe she could make a run for the bridge and . . . and what? Throw herself over the side?

They stood together for a moment, in silence.

'Right . . . well . . .' said Alfi. 'I guess we'd—'

'Let's go,' said Roskva. 'Jotunheim is a long, long way from here.'

'Noooooo!' wailed Freya. 'I can't do this!'

Snot picked her up and slung her over his back as if she were a sack of wool. She kicked and wailed and wept as they hurried on their way.

4 The River Irving

'Put me down!' shrieked Freya. She pounded Snot's gnarled back and beat his chest with her feet.

Snot ignored her.

Freya felt her streaming nose squash into her face as it bang-bang-banged against Snot's back as he stomped across the withered meadows outside Asgard's great wall, trailed by Roskva and Alfi. The stench from his matted bear-shirt and cloak was horrible.

'I said put me down!' screamed Freya. She tried not

to breathe in his stink.

'Is this how you want your saga to end?' said Snot fiercely. 'Crying and mewling? After the sword, or sickness, or old age ends your life, only reputation lives on.'

'I don't care about my saga!' said Freya. She started weeping again. 'I want to go home.'

'Well, you can't and neither can we, so ACCEPT YOUR FATE,' screamed Roskva. She muttered under her breath to Alfi.

Freya stopped crying.

Accept her fate? She was under sentence of death. Wolves? Trolls? Giants? If they didn't kill her, other monsters would. And if by luck she escaped them, the wilderness would snare her and she'd drown in a river or tumble off a mountain. And even if fate decreed that she survive, what was the chance of finding Idunn and bringing her back to Asgard before nine nights ran out? Nil.

Strangely enough, Freya felt calmer spelling this out. No one knows their fate, she thought, wiping her eyes. If I only have nine more days to live then I'd better make the best of them.

'I can walk, you know,' she said. 'Put me down.'

'Then stop whimpering,' barked Snot, dumping her

on the gravelly ground. Freya sat up, rubbing her arm where she'd landed.

Outside the ghostly ruined citadel of the Gods, the afternoon sun lit up the vast plains. There was no sound except the roar of a tumultuous river. When had she last slept? She couldn't remember.

'Are all girls like you now?' said Roskva, looking down at her with distaste. 'You're very soft. Where's your spirit of adventure?'

My spirit of adventure is trying a new vegetable, thought Freya. She didn't dare say it out loud.

'Don't give up hope, Freya,' said Alfi. He smiled at her and helped her to her feet. 'I've done this sort of thing before.'

'Yeah, with Thor behind you all the way,' said Roskva.

'We'll be back with Idunn before you know it,' said Alfi.

Freya stared at him.

'How can you be so cheerful?' said Freya, scowling.

'A man should be happy until his dying day,' said Alfi, shifting restlessly from foot to foot. 'My grandpa used to say it's always better to live than lie dead.'

Yeah right, thought Freya. Good for your grandpa. She gnawed on her frayed sleeve.

Roskva whistled. Freya heard pounding hooves, and Sleipnir galloped over, snorting, his eight legs churning the stony ground.

'Hurry up!' said Snot, striding towards the gleaming river. 'We want to get as far as we can before nightfall.'

'Snot! You're going the wrong way,' shouted Alfi. 'Jotunheim is north-east. We need to head for the mountains past the River Irving.'

Snot stalked over to Alfi. He towered over him.

'Are you as brave as me?' he bellowed. His crooked brows bristled.

'Far from it,' said Alfi, cowering.

Snot kicked Alfi's feet from under him. Alfi fell over.

'Just remember that and we'll get on fine,' said Snot. 'Don't you tell me which way to go. *I'm* leading this quest.'

'Says who?' said Roskva.

'Says me,' said Snot. 'I am Woden's chosen warrior.'

'We've all been chosen,' said Roskva.

'Actually, I think Freya is leader,' mumbled Alfi. 'She blew Heimdall's horn.'

'What?' said Snot. He looked like he was about to attack Alfi again.

'*She's* our leader?' said Roskva. Her eyes flashed.

I'm leader? thought Freya. If she thought it would do any good she would have howled. No one had ever asked her to lead anything. I'm a follower, thought Freya. I'm Betty the brunette, the leader's best friend. Not—

'I should be leader,' said Roskva. 'I'm the smartest.'

Snot glared at them. 'I take orders from no one but Woden. And certainly not from children.'

'For the last time we are not children!' screamed Roskva.

Freya looked at the furious faces around her. Sleipnir snorted and stamped the ground, eager to go. We haven't even set off and already we're fighting, she thought.

'So go on, Freya, tell us, what makes you so special?' said Roskva. 'You wear no rings or gold arm bracelets so you must be poor and without protectors. You're small. You're very plain. You can't even walk on Bifrost without vomiting. And yet the Gods have chosen you and Alfi thinks you should lead us. Are you a seeress?'

'No,' said Freya. At least she didn't think she was.

'Then what's so special about you?' Roskva repeated.

Freya tried to focus.

'Nothing,' said Freya.

What talents did she have? Did she even have any?

75

She'd been in her school's 'Good as Gold' book twice in a row. She held the school record for the most pancakes eaten in ten minutes. And she could . . . and she had . . . Somehow Freya didn't think being good as gold or able to stuff her face with pancakes was going to help her much now. How depressing to be twelve years old and good at nothing.

'What are *you* good at?' asked Freya.

'I'm the fastest runner in Midgard,' said Alfi. 'Well, I was. I imagine I still am. I'm certainly the oldest.' He grinned.

'I'm almost as fast as you,' said Roskva hotly. 'And let's face it. I'm a lot smarter.'

'A quick tongue often talks itself into trouble,' said Alfi.

'And out of it,' said Roskva.

Freya felt as if she were watching a ping-pong match between brother and sister.

'We must go NOW,' bellowed Snot. His fists clenched. 'We have to travel as far as possible before dark.'

Freya saw the others looking at her expectantly.

'I don't want to be leader,' said Freya, trembling. 'I don't know my way around . . . I don't know anything, really . . . But . . . but . . . can I just ask . . . has anyone

ever been where we're going? To the land of the giants?
Jot – Jot—'

'Jotunheim,' said Roskva. 'Alfi and I have been many
times with our Master. It's north-east from here.
The River Irving marks the boundary. Ever been to
Jotunheim, Snot?'

Snot looked down at her and bit his shield. He said
nothing.

'Thought so,' said Roskva.

Snot's hand tightened on his sword.

'You're lucky that Woden ordered me to protect
you,' he snarled.

'Then I think Alfi and Roskva should guide us
there,' said Freya. 'We can argue about who is leader
later. Does anyone have a better plan?'

'That's settled then,' said Roskva, without waiting
for anyone to answer. She grabbed hold of Sleipnir's
golden bridle. 'Four can ride at once,' she said. 'If we
squeeze.'

Freya held back. Horses terrified her.

She stared up at Sleipnir. The gleaming grey horse
towered over her. He was longer and wider than any
horse she'd ever seen.

'I've never ridden before,' said Freya.

'High time you did,' said Roskva, clambering on.

Snot heaved her unceremoniously on to Sleipnir behind Roskva. Freya scrabbled about and tried to swing her legs over his broad back without slipping over the other side. The ground looked very far away. Snot hesitated, then climbed on behind Freya, muttering and growling. Alfi sprang on last, vaulting easily over Sleipnir's tail.

'AAEEEEEEE!' screamed Freya, as Sleipnir galloped off. 'Help,' she squealed. 'I'm going to fall!'

She clung frantically to Roskva and squeezed her eyes shut as Sleipnir jumped the flinty river as if it were a puddle and scrambled up the opposite bank.

'Careful, you'll pull me off!' shouted Roskva as Freya clutched her waist, terrified, rocking and jolting on top of the speeding horse.

Soon the plains and parched meadows of Asgard were behind them. Freya sat squished between Roskva and Snot, her eyes squeezed shut every time Sleipnir leapt over a river or a lake, her knees gripping his smooth sides as tightly as she could as they vaulted through the air, landing with a horrendous bump that made Freya's stomach lurch. Far, far away, she could see mountains black with forest, lost in grey clouds.

For hour after hour they crossed river valleys and hillsides, wooded below, rocky higher up. Waterfalls tumbled down sheer, pink-grey cliffs, flowing over boulders into frothy pools. Freya dared to open her eyes for a time and glimpsed tiny blue flowers growing between the rocks littering the overgrown path. Sleipnir crushed them underfoot.

Freya was concentrating so hard on not falling off she barely looked where they were going. It was difficult to talk, they were travelling so fast. Roskva's long hair, tied back in a knot at her neck, kept whacking Freya's face.

'What's that?' shouted Freya. She pointed to a huge, monstrous-shaped stone, squatting by the steep, winding path between the hills they were crossing. The arms were outstretched, like a bulbous Valkyrie of the North.

Roskva shrugged. 'Petrified troll,' she said. 'They get sun on them – bam! They turn to stone. Our Master tricked one once – Alviss.'

'Good times,' shouted Alfi.

Freya shook her head. Poor Alfi. What a dreadful life he'd led, if tricking trolls was his idea of fun.

The wind whistled through the valley as shadows started to drift across their path. The snowy peaks of the giants' icy lands loomed in the distance behind small hills rolling off into the horizon. Freya heard the clamour of a fast-flowing river and caught the glint of silvery water through the scented pine trees.

'That's the boundary,' said Roskva.

Freya didn't need to ask which one.

'We need a place to camp,' said Snot, scrambling to be first off Sleipnir. These were the first words he'd spoken since they'd set off. 'We'll stay on the Asgard side of the river. It's too dangerous to travel at night. We'll cross into Jotunheim at dawn.'

It was a plan. Freya liked plans, and to-do lists, and re-doing homework in neat and someone in charge telling her what to do. That way she knew where she was. Unfortunately, where she was wasn't anything she could have planned for.

Freya slid the long way down from Sleipnir and watched the giant horse trot through the tangled trees to the river to gulp great mouthfuls of water. Her legs wobbled and muscles she never knew she had felt battered and bruised. All she wanted to do was to stretch out somewhere, anywhere, and sleep. A strange thought, as camping was her idea of Hel.

Alfi found a little green gully which provided some shelter from the wind. Snot nodded. 'That'll do,' he said. Alfi flung himself to the ground, amidst coarse clumps of rough grass, breathing hard. Roskva bustled about, tending to Sleipnir, the stallion glowing in the forest's olive light.

Freya felt helpless. She was useless at games, useless at climbing. She was clumsy. She hated PE. Get a good education, Mum and Dad were always telling her. But she would have been better off just being physically fit and never picking up a book, she thought bitterly as she skidded on the mossy stones littering the slimy river bank to get some water to drink. Maybe there was a good reason why museums were always putting up signs saying 'Don't touch'.

It was eerily quiet. Freya hated nature, so cold, so wet, so uncomfortable, so malevolent. She always felt nervous off concrete. Her whole body ached. I'm hungry, she thought. Do these people eat?

Freya stood on the banks of the wide, sparkling river separating Asgard from Jotunheim. She thought for a moment to dip her feet in, but the boiling current changed her mind. Scooping up the clear, icy water in her cupped hands, Freya drank, shuddering at the cold.

She glimpsed the far-away, jagged mountains, and grim gulches and gulleys, lit by the dying rays of the sun. The flat-peaked mountains looked like a giant had taken a gigantic saw and lopped off their tops.

A giant probably did take a gigantic saw and lop off their tops, thought Freya.

Roskva pointed.

'Jotunheim,' she said. 'It gets much worse further in.'

'Worse?' said Freya.

'Jotunheim is a biting land of gales and rock and ice,' said Roskva. 'And that's the good bit. Where Thjazi lives . . . it's so cold the air aches.'

Great, thought Freya. Just great. Can't wait to freeze to death before I'm eaten alive.

'I'll find food before it gets too dark,' said Snot. 'You—' he pointed to Alfi. 'Keep your hand on your sword. And no one goes to pee alone.'

Freya watched Snot slip down to the river bank and disappear around a bend.

'He smells,' she said.

'No he doesn't,' said Roskva, gathering up twigs and pieces of kindling lying thick amidst the dead bracken and mossy undergrowth. 'On the other hand, *you* smell . . .'

'Me?'

'You. Sort of . . . sickly-sweet. Ugh.' Roskva wrinkled her nose.

'That's deodorant,' said Freya.

'What?'

'Stops you smelling,' said Freya.

Roskva looked at her. 'Why don't you just take a bath?'

'I do that too,' said Freya hotly.

'I haven't had a bath in . . . a long time,' said Roskva. 'We had our own bathhouse at home, with a stone floor, and little benches . . . Tyrsday was bath day . . .' She shook her head and bent over her kindling.

Freya watched Roskva and Alfi prepare a fire. Roskva struck a light with a piece of flint strung on her belt. The tiny spark flickered, then the kindling caught.

'Why did Thor take you from your parents?' asked Freya, as the tiny flames spluttered into life.

'Why don't you ask *him*?' said Roskva. 'It's his fault.'

Alfi's face darkened. 'By Thor, would you stop it?'

'I was happy on our farm,' said Roskva. 'I never wanted anything more.'

'Oh Gods, here we go again,' groaned Alfi. 'For the last time, I was *hungry*.'

Roskva continued as if he hadn't spoken.

'But no, you had to disobey Thor when he stopped at our home and slaughtered his magic goat for us to eat. He said over and over, "Be careful with the bones, throw them *whole* onto the goat's skin," but no, you greedy guts, you had to gnaw the leg bone and crack it,

83

the goat was lame when Thor brought it back to life, and then it was scream and beg for mercy and goodbye Mum, goodbye Dad, goodbye little farm, hello being a bondservant for ever and ever to atone for the wrong *you* did. Not me. You.'

'The Mighty One showed great mercy when he spared our lives.'

'Some mercy,' said Roskva. 'He just torments us now instead of killing us then.'

'Our farm was a dump,' said Alfi. 'Remember the stink? Remember how lonely it was? Remember that turf roof with the rats scrabbling about?'

'I miss Mum,' she said. 'I even miss the cows.'

'Mum's been dead for thousands of years,' said Alfi. 'And Dad. And so would you be if Thor hadn't taken us.'

Roskva sighed loudly.

'At least I'd have *had* a life.'

'No one can escape their fate,' said Alfi.

'I hope it's my fate to kill you,' said Roskva. She punched him lightly on the arm.

Alfi laughed.

'And yours to be the mother of ogres.'

'Meanie.'

But she smiled briefly as she blew on the embers. The flames crackled.

84

'Where's that berserk gone?' muttered Roskva. 'I'm hungry.'

'What exactly does berserk mean?' asked Freya.

'It means we love a good fight,' said Snot, appearing through the growing gloom carrying a dripping salmon speared on his sword. He whacked the quivering fish on the ground and chopped off its head. His eyes glinted in the firelight. Then he took out his knife and started hacking the fish into large chunks. He stuffed one raw into his mouth. 'We are priests of war. When I fight I join the Gods. I feel no pain. Nothing can—'

Snot growled. He whipped off his cloak and beat out the flames.

'Hey!' said Roskva. 'I—'

'Get down!' he hissed.

Freya froze.

'Get down,' said Alfi, pulling her.

They flung themselves into the sweet-smelling bracken.

'Don't move,' said Snot.

'What? What is it?' whispered Freya.

'Above us,' muttered Roskva.

Freya looked. High overhead, an eagle circled the darkening sky.

'It's just an eagle,' said Freya. 'How can he harm us?'

'The giant Thjazi can take the form of an eagle,' said Roskva. The huge bird circled above them, its immense wings etched against the night sky.

'The horse. He might have seen the horse,' said Freya.

'So?' said Alfi. 'It's the All-Father's horse. No great surprise seeing Sleipnir around Asgard.'

'Let's hope he didn't,' said Roskva.

The mighty eagle circled again, then, screeching, flew off back into the dark hills.

'He's gone,' said Roskva, standing up and brushing herself off. 'We can pray he didn't see us. Now make yourself useful, Freya, and collect some wood,' she added brusquely, re-lighting the fire. Freya noticed Roskva's hands were shaking.

Freya gathered whatever pieces of wood were nearest and added them to the small heap by the fire. No way was she going into the forest alone.

'Do you think that was Thjazi?' said Freya. She felt terrified.

Roskva shrugged. 'It could have been an ordinary eagle. Or . . .'

'I'll kill Thjazi in single combat,' snarled Snot. His sharp sword gleamed. 'I am a warrior from Valhalla.' He threw a salmon chunk at Alfi.

86

'Get sticks. Roast them yourselves.'

Freya looked at the bloody hunks of raw fish piled up by the fire. Her stomach heaved.

'Umm. I don't like fish,' said Freya.

'Then you won't eat,' said Roskva, threading a chunk of fish onto a stick and holding it above the flames.

'One of my sons was a fussy eater,' said Snot. 'Not for long . . .' His fingers played on his blood-washed sword. He sat with his back to them, weapons by his side, his body tense and watchful.

Freya squared her shoulders and forced herself to touch a piece of salmon with the tips of her fingers. Ugh. So slimy. She impaled it on a stick, then sat down with Roskva and Alfi. Part of her wanted to scream, how can you talk about food when we're about to be eaten?

The moon rose, casting a faint light. At least there's still a moon, she thought.

'Why do you think Loki never came back to Asgard?' said Freya. Talking made her feel less scared.

Roskva grimaced. 'Who knows? Maybe he couldn't. Maybe he got trapped by Thjazi. Maybe he wouldn't. Maybe he's dead.'

'Loki is a shape-changer,' said Alfi. 'It's impossible to know his true nature. One moment he is playful and fun, the next cruel and strange.'

'You know what they say about him?' said Roskva. 'That come the end of days Loki will lead the armies of the dead and the giants and destroy Asgard.'

Freya shook her head. 'I was taught Loki rescued Idunn and saved the Gods. And that was — a lie. What else is lies?'

No one answered.

Alfi mixed some grains in a small iron pot he'd taken from Sleipnir's saddle-bag and filled with river water. He sniffed something, grimaced, and put it back in the pouch.

'Aren't you going to cook that?' said Roskva.

'Why?' said Alfi. 'At least it's barley flour. We'll be eating stale oat cakes and rotten herring and acorns soon so enjoy this while you can.'

Alfi slopped a spoonful of stuff into Freya's hands.

She looked at the thin, watery glop. It was grey and sticky and lumpy. It looked like — it looked like — Freya didn't want to think what it looked like. She sniffed it, then wished she hadn't.

'What is this?' she asked.

'Gruel,' said Roskva, slurping up a huge mouthful.

Gruel?

Gruel sounded a lot like what Oliver Twist wanted

more of. Gruel sounded like something you ate in Victorian England along with rats and old shoes.

'How old is it?' said Freya. She had a horrible feeling it might be past its sell-by date. Way past its sell-by date.

Roskva shrugged. 'How old is Yggdrasil? How old is that mountain? How old? How old? It's food. Eat it.'

Freya had a sudden memory of pushing away her dinner because her corn on the cob had touched her roast chicken. She liked to eat things on separate plates. She shoved the lumpy, horrible-tasting mess into her mouth and swallowed as quickly as she could. Then she picked up her stick of salmon and held it over the fire.

Snot slurped up his gruel in three quick gulps. Then he sat sharpening his huge sword blade.

Alfi flinched. 'That sounds worse than someone edging a scythe on a stone,' he said.

'You don't like it, block your ears,' grunted Snot.

'One thing I don't understand,' said Freya. 'Why would Loki give Idunn to a giant?'

'Why. Why. Why. Gods, do you ever stop asking questions?' muttered Snot. He rolled his eyes.

'Loki attacked an eagle who turned out to be the giant Thjazi in disguise,' said Roskva. 'Thjazi grabbed

Loki and smashed him into boulders and thorns until Loki swore he would bring Idunn to him.'

'Why did Loki keep his promise?' said Freya.

'You must understand something,' said Alfi. 'Loki's father was a giant. So. Is he loyal to the Gods? Or to the giants?'

'The Gods do what they like,' said Roskva. 'We mortals live with the consequences.' She and Alfi looked at one another in silence.

'The Valkyries snatched me from battle,' said Snot. 'I was fighting. *I* was winning. But Woden sent the Choosers of the Slain to take *me* and not the filthy son of a mare I was walloping.' He shrugged. 'If a man knew his fate he'd go mad.'

'Your fish is burning,' said Roskva.

Wrinkling her nose at the acrid smell, Freya withdrew the blackened chunk. Tentatively she took a tiny bite. The flesh was burnt on the outside, and raw on the inside. She forced herself to eat a bit more, her stomach heaving.

Freya felt them before she heard it. A thin, deep-pitched, hungry howl. And then another. And another.

Her skin prickled. She whimpered and edged closer to the fire. The other three grabbed flaming sticks and stood with their backs to the heat, facing outward.

Freya caught a glimpse of glowing amber-red eyes. She had no idea what to do. Roskva pulled out her knife.

Snot ran bellowing into the trees, brandishing the burning wood and wielding his sword. Alfi hesitated and drew his sword, uncertain whether to follow or stay.

'Oh, give me that,' screamed Roskva, snatching his blade and edging towards the forest.

'Oy! I was just about to—' spluttered Alfi, grabbing it back, when Snot reappeared from the darkness.

'The wolves have gone,' said Snot. The firelight glistened on his bloody sword. 'But not for long. We'll keep watch tonight. Now that they've smelt us, they won't leave us.'

They huddled close together by the fire, the night around them thick and black as the clouds hid the half-moon. Freya bit her lip hard to stop herself bursting into tears.

'Anyone know any poetry?' said Alfi. His voice trembled. 'What about Egil Skallagrimsson?'

'Who?' said Freya. Her voice was also shaky.

'You've never heard of him?' said Alfi.

'Nope,' said Freya.

'Unbelievable,' said Alfi. 'What about Eyvind the Plagiarist?'

Freya shook her head. 'I know a bit of Shakespeare

. . . we studied *Hamlet* in school.' Her voice quavering, she recited:

> *To be or not to be; that is the question:*
> *whether 'tis nobler in the mind to suffer—*

'Who?' interrupted Roskva. 'He's terrible.'

'What about Audun the Uninspired?' said Snot. 'I always liked Audun.'

'Let's hear it,' said Alfi.

Snot stood, sword drawn, left hand on his hip, and recited, his gravelly voice low:

> *Oh battle bright warrior*
> *How the gold of your brooch-goddess gleams*
> *Too soon raven's food litters the blood-soaked ground*
> *Wolf's teeth stained with blood.*

Alfi clapped. His sword, Freya noticed, was clutched tight in his hand.

'Do you know anything more cheerful?' said Freya. The thought of bloody wolf's teeth was a little close to home at the moment.

'Cheerful!' Snot spat. He thought for a moment. 'There's always that funny poem of Eyvind's . . .

My sword, flame of battle
Digs deep in enemy ribs.
Wound-sea pours red from the trailing guts
My shield-splitting arm
Hacks him to pieces
Ready for the eagle's snack.

Snot laughed. It sounded more like a rasp than a laugh.

'It's good, no? I especially like the phrase "eagle's snack".' He hesitated for a moment. 'I write a bit of poetry myself.'

'Go on,' said Roskva.

'I'm no Eyvind . . .'

And then Snot stood up again, threw back his grizzled head, and recited:

Eagle food
Raven food
Warriors all end up as bloody food.
When you're a wolf meal
No point in gold then
A dead man gathers no wealth inside the wolf's belly.

'True,' said Alfi.

AAAAAARRRRGGGHHHH! thought Freya.

Did every poem have to be about being eaten by eagles and wolves?

Snot glowered. 'You don't need to pretend. I didn't say I was a good poet, I said I wrote a bit of poetry. But a king did give me the gift of my own head once for that verse.'

Alfi looked puzzled.

'He pardoned him,' said Roskva.

Snot smiled faintly. 'I think I must have been happy then.'

They were silent. Freya watched the flames and listened to the howling river. Her shoulders tensed. Any moment a giant could burst out of the darkness and trample them to death. Or a wolf could tear them to pieces. She could feel her heart banging against her chest, its quick-quick beats reverberating inside her. How could the others be so calm when they could be killed at any moment?

'Roskva, what charms did the All-Father give you?' asked Alfi, poking the fire.

'Calming waves,' said Roskva.

'I can tell men the names of all the Gods and all the elves one by one,' said Alfi.

'That'll be a help against Thjazi,' said Roskva. 'Maybe he'll challenge you to a naming contest and whoever wins gets Idunn.'

Alfi brightened.

'Do you think so?' he said.

'NO!' said Roskva. 'Only stupid dwarfs fall for that one.'

'You never know what's going to help,' said Alfi. 'What about you, Snot?'

Snot spat.

'I can quench any fire,' said Snot. 'He could have taught me how to blunt an enemy's sword, or how to strengthen a band of comrades so they walk unscathed from battle. But no. I'm a bloody fire-fighter.' He spat again.

'If I see a hanged man in a tree I can make him come down and talk to me,' said Freya. She shivered. 'Oh wait. I didn't get anything. The All-Father forgot the last part of the rune.'

'You got the falcon skin,' said Roskva.

'So I did,' said Freya. Her fingers felt in her pocket for the feather. Her eyes felt heavy.

Alfi was also struggling to keep awake.

'We should sleep,' said Snot. 'I'll take first watch.'

Alfi wrapped himself in his cloak and stretched out by the crackling fire. 'Oh, my aching legs,' he murmured, pulling off his hairy leather ankle boots and rubbing his pale feet.

There was a strangled cry.

'Roskva!' he said. 'Look.'

Freya stared. There was some sort of creamy chalk on both Alfi's feet up to his ankles. He tried to rub it off, but the mottled colour remained.

Roskva took off her boots.

'It's happening to me too,' said Roskva quietly.

Her heart pounding, Freya pulled off her own shoes and socks. There was the same mottled ivory-brown colour creeping up her feet to her ankles. She touched her toes. They felt exactly the same, but they tingled, and her skin had changed colour.

'What's happening to us?' whispered Freya.

'I think . . . I think we're slowly turning back into ivory,' said Roskva. 'Bit by bit. If we haven't restored Idunn to the Gods by the ninth night—'

She didn't need to complete the sentence.

'We don't know that,' said Freya. 'It might be something else. It might be gone by morning.'

'It might,' said Roskva. She fixed Freya with a dark look. 'And Sleipnir might talk.'

Roskva spread her heavy cloak on the ground, sat down on one side and beckoned to Freya. 'Here. We can share.'

Freya hesitated. The night wasn't cold, but she had nothing to put on the ground.

'Thanks,' she said.

Alfi already lay snoring beside them. His pale bare feet stuck out from the end of the cloak he'd wrapped himself in. Snot sat brooding over the fire, poking at the embers and singing tunelessly: 'Thor's lost his hammer/ Oh look it's in your head.'

Freya gazed at the glittering stars studding the blue-black sky. They didn't look like any stars she'd ever seen before, grouped in unfamiliar patterns. Her parents would never know what had happened to her. Bob would do his rounds, maybe peer into the case housing the Lewis Chessmen, never realising that . . . that . . .

I won't think about it, she decided. I'll just try to get through tonight and hope I survive tomorrow.

Freya huddled down on the dusty fur and tried to get comfortable. It was impossible. She needed to sleep in a bed. She could feel stones dig into her back.

Freya tossed and twisted. Tears stung her eyes. She'd never get to sleep.

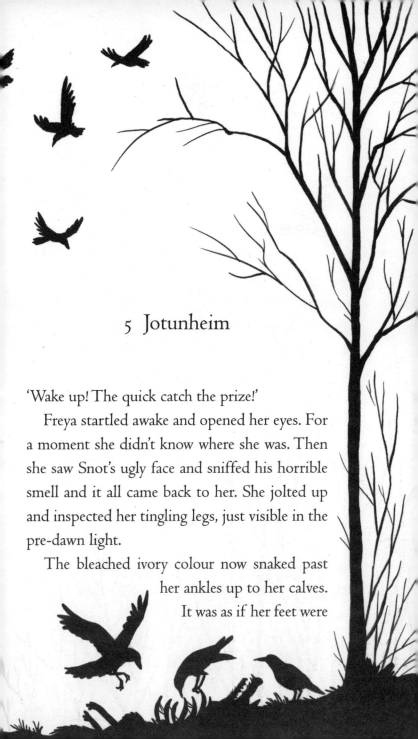

5 Jotunheim

'Wake up! The quick catch the prize!'

Freya startled awake and opened her eyes. For a moment she didn't know where she was. Then she saw Snot's ugly face and sniffed his horrible smell and it all came back to her. She jolted up and inspected her tingling legs, just visible in the pre-dawn light.

The bleached ivory colour now snaked past her ankles up to her calves. It was as if her feet were already corpses. Freya trembled.

Roskva and Alfi were already up and Sleipnir, steaming and glistening, saddled. His eight legs were mottled-ivory to the knees. The early dawn sky was tinged pinky-orange on the edges of the horizon. Restless ravens circled overhead crying *kraa kraa kraa* and wisps of mist rose from the chilly ground. The damp air smelled faintly of pine.

'We want to cross into Jotunheim as quietly as possible,' said Roskva. 'If we get over the River Irving now, we can hopefully reach the forest without being seen.'

Alfi crammed a few acorns and berries into his mouth. Roskva gnawed on some wild leeks. Snot ate some dried fish that looked like stiff dirt.

Roskva opened Sleipnir's saddlebag and rooted around inside.

'Eat,' said Roskva, passing her a crumbling pre-historic oat cake.

Freya was about to say she wasn't a breakfast person but decided not to. The oat cake tasted like dusty cardboard. Freya slipped the remains into her pocket. Her fingers touched a bar of chocolate. She gazed at the smooth red wrapper. No. She'd keep it for later. She felt something smooth and round, and her face flushed. It was the silvery pot of pink lip gloss she'd bought with her pocket money.

Clare forbade her to wear make-up so Freya always kept it hidden. She also found her squeaky duck keyring which emitted a tiny light when she pressed the beak, the ugly tortoiseshell hair clip Clare liked her to wear, and her black mobile phone. She put the clip into her hair, then pulled out the mobile.

Dead. What had she expected?

'What's that?' said Alfi.

'My phone,' said Freya. 'It doesn't work here.'

'Ah,' he said. 'I always wondered . . . in the place of dead things people were always talking into them, like madmen mumbling to themselves.'

Freya heard wings flapping. Instinctively, she ducked. Then she saw what had drawn the carrion birds: the ravens were tearing at the bodies of two slaughtered wolves. Freya averted her eyes. That could have been me, she thought.

They slipped down to the water's edge and mounted Sleipnir. Freya looked out across the silvery river to pebbly banks, wreathed with scrub, sloping uphill to the thick, clustered trees which she could just make out in the pale light.

She felt Sleipnir brace himself, then Woden's horse vaulted over the bright river separating Asgard and Jotunheim. He failed to clear it entirely and they landed with a gigantic splash before scrambling up the rocky wasteland which lay between the river and the bleak forest looming ahead.

Freya shivered. The temperature was noticeably colder and the air was damp and chill. Everything felt menacing, as if the still land was holding its breath waiting for the explosion which would rip them to pieces. The stagnant air smelled stale and strange.

She kept her eyes fixed on the forest ahead, half-expecting to see a giant come striding out to challenge them.

'Which way?' said Alfi, surveying the grim land under the leaden sky.

Is he looking for a road sign? thought Freya. 'Thrymheim this way?'

'Towards those mountains . . .' said Roskva. 'The squat ones over there. Honestly, do I have to do everything for you?'

'I remember perfectly how to get there,' said Alfi. 'I was just getting my bearings.'

'Yeah right,' said Roskva.

'You can be such an old herring sometimes,' muttered Alfi.

'Speak for yourself, sardine breath.'

'Fish face.'

'You stinking mare's son!'

'I hope the trolls get you!'

'Shut up!' bellowed Snot. 'Or by Thor I'll bite both your heads off.'

'I thought we were supposed to be keeping quiet,' said Freya. She looked around anxiously.

Roskva glared. 'Do you have a younger brother?'

'No,' said Freya.

'Fate was kind to you there,' said Roskva. She kicked Sleipnir hard and he charged off.

'I had brothers,' said Snot suddenly. 'And a wife. She was as beautiful to look at as my axe inlaid with oak. Well. She's long returned to the trolls.'

Freya didn't know what to say. She couldn't imagine Snot with a family.

Sleipnir galloped inland, his hooves crunching on the pine-needle-strewn path, scaling the cliffs as easily as if they were meadows. In the distance Freya could see a range of low black mountains jutting against the horizon, squashed by the heavy sky.

Then the trees swallowed them up and they were in a dark, silent forest of pine and birch. The ground was boggy, covered with dead leaves and dense undergrowth. The track glistened with frost, and bright green mossy rocks loomed out of the cliffs.

Fallen trees and vicious brambles frequently blocked their path, which had clearly not been travelled on for a long time. Louring clouds hid the faint sun. They searched the sky anxiously, but the eagle didn't reappear.

The further they travelled, the greyer and stormier it became. The only sound was the harsh shriek of ravens and the howling cry of wolves. Freya had never felt like something's dinner before. The evil air was oppressive. Freya found herself breathing in short, shallow gasps. She couldn't get over the feeling that they were being watched and tracked as they rode ever higher into the brooding mountains.

'How long till we get to Thjazi's?' she asked. Part of her never wanted to get there, then she caught a glimpse of the ivory creeping above her falling knee socks and she wanted Sleipnir to gallop even faster.

'At least another night,' said Alfi. 'His storm-home is deep within Jotunheim.'

'What do we do if we meet a giant or a troll on the way?' said Freya.

Alfi shrugged. 'We'll say we're travelling to . . . to visit a friend.'

'And they'll believe that?'

'We'll just have to keep our wits about us,' said

Roskva. 'Giants are unpredictable. Oww!' she wailed, as a low-hanging branch whacked her head. 'How come I always have to sit in front and get thorns in my face?' she snapped, brushing aside another bramble. 'Whoa, Sleipnir,' she shouted, slowing down the horse so that she could disentangle her cloak and hair from the prickly thorns dangling from trees on either side of the narrow path.

'That's because you like sitting in front,' said Alfi.

'You go first and see how you like it.'

'Okay, I will,' said Alfi.

'Be my guest,' said Roskva. 'I can't do everything.'

'No one's asking you to,' said Freya.

Roskva ignored her.

'Who cleaned the horse last night? He's got EIGHT hooves, remember?' said Roskva. 'I dug mud and leaves and muck out of EIGHT hooves.'

'Who did the cooking?' said Alfi.

'Call that cooking? Shoving a few grisly bits in a pot and stirring them?'

'You ate it . . .'

'I can help next time,' said Freya.

Roskva turned on her. 'Can you look after a horse?'

'No,' said Freya. 'But I can—'

'Can you cook?' interrupted Roskva, yanking her

hair free and dropping the bramble on the ground.

I can microwave a pizza, thought Freya. I can open a tin of soup. Clare didn't like her messing up the kitchen, and Bob always ordered in whenever she stayed over.

'Umm, not really,' she said. 'I can follow a recipe . . .' Somehow she didn't think a Jamie Oliver cookbook was going to pop out of Sleipnir's saddlebag.

'A *recipe*?' said Roskva. 'What's that?'

'It tells you how to make things like chicken or cakes, what ingredients to use . . .'

Roskva stared at her.

'What's there to know? Get a pot, fill it with water, boil up whatever you've got. The end. A *recipe*?! You do live in soft times. So what *can* you do? Your mother must have taught you to brew ale and milk ewes and gut fish . . .'

'Not exactly,' said Freya. She smiled at the thought of her Mum milking a sheep. 'I don't live on a farm.'

'Neither do I,' said Roskva. 'Not any more.'

'Thank the Gods,' murmured Alfi.

'Can we get a move on?' said Snot. '*I'll* sit in front. Roskva, keep watch behind us.'

They rode hard all day, through whispering forests and craggy wastelands, and the next, the air getting colder and stormier the deeper they travelled into Jotunheim. Freya felt as if they were galloping towards her death. They met no one.

'You can travel for days in these lands without meeting anyone,' said Alfi. '*If* you're lucky.'

Freya couldn't stop checking her numb legs, watching in horrified fascination as the mottled ivory colour crept upwards, fraction by fraction. It was like a scab she couldn't stop picking. Had it reached the scar above her knee yet? When would it pass the birthmark on her thigh?

As the light started to fade on the third day, a freezing mist sprang up, wrapping them in its sticky embrace. Then it began to sleet. A bitter wind blew the icy rain in their faces.

Freya shivered. The dampness ate into her bones.

It was getting harder and harder to see through the twilight. Sleipnir slowed to a walk as he picked his way through dense copses and thickets, his hooves squelching on the boggy ground. He was breathing hard and his ears kept pricking, as if he were hearing something. Freya could feel his body trembling beneath her aching legs.

'There are wolves hunting us,' said Snot. He stiffened. 'If we can, we should find shelter for the night.'

'I'll see what I can find,' said Alfi.

'Wait,' said Freya. 'Don't go alone. What if the wolves—'

'Don't worry,' shouted Alfi, dashing off into the forest.

He was back again so quickly that Freya only blinked a few times.

'I've found a glade not too far up ahead, with an empty hall in the middle,' he panted.

'How do you know it's empty?' said Roskva. 'Did you dare go inside?'

Alfi glowered.

'No.'

'Didn't think so,' said Roskva.

'It's empty,' said Alfi.

The others followed him to the clearing and gawped at the building, looming gigantic and black in the moonlight.

'It's bigger than Valhalla,' muttered Snot.

There was no door, but the wide opening was as high as the hall itself.

'Will the wolves follow us in here?' asked Freya as they crept inside out of the sleet, swords drawn.

'Depends how hungry they are,' said Snot.

The main hall was empty. There was no furniture, not even a table or chair. Just a vast, barren chamber. Freya felt for a moment that she was inside Woden's great temple in All-Father Square.

Off to the right, about halfway down, was a smaller side hall, pitch-dark and airless. At the end were passageways leading to smaller halls. There was no furniture, or hangings, or even a hearth. It smelled musty, as if it hadn't been lived in for a long time, and the floor was rough and uneven. They heard hailstones pounding on the roof. Freya stumbled and brushed her hands against the wall. She'd expected to feel cold smooth stone, but it was surprisingly lumpy and, in places, almost spongy.

'It's warmer and drier in here than out there,' said Roskva, almost invisible in the darkness. 'And no wolves. I say we stay.'

Freya was so cold and weary and worn out with travel she would have gladly sheltered anywhere dry. Her teeth chattered. She felt something heavy and furry draped over her shoulders.

'Take it,' said Snot gruffly, fastening his heavy cloak with an iron studded brooch. 'I don't feel the cold. Or pain. Or anything.'

The bear fur smelled abominable, but Freya was too cold at that moment to care. The cloak fell to her ankles, dragging behind her like some monstrous train.

'Thank you,' said Freya.

Snot shook his head. 'This isn't for you. I don't care if you live or die. I swore to Woden that I would protect you and I will fulfil my oath.'

'Oh,' said Freya. Gods, she hated him. When his back was turned she stuck out her tongue and made a horrible gargoyle face.

They settled in the murky side hall, and ate quickly. Freya didn't even ask, she just put the dried, salty whatever-it-was in her mouth and chewed. Fish and chips. With lashings of ketchup. What she would give for a pepperoni pizza dripping with melted mozzarella and some hot buttery garlic bread . . .

She checked her tingling legs and saw that the mottled ivory had snaked above her thighs, creeping upwards to her hips. How could her legs have turned ivory so quickly? She could almost feel the creamy tendrils inching up her body.

No one seemed to feel much like talking.

'So . . . tomorrow . . . Thrymheim,' said Alfi.

'Umm, any plans?' said Freya.

'We'll try to sneak in when Thjazi's not there,' said Alfi.

'But how will we get inside his house?' said Freya.

'We'll have to find a way,' said Alfi.

'We need to be clever,' said Roskva. 'Giants are . . . giants. They're much bigger and stronger than we are.'

'Duh,' said Freya.

'It's always best to avoid a fight with them,' said Alfi.

Snot snorted. 'Coward,' he muttered.

Freya glared at him. Then she realised he probably couldn't see her in the darkness, so she glared harder.

'That's not being a coward,' said Freya. 'That's being . . . clever.'

'Anyway I'm not a coward,' said Alfi. 'Remember who frightened that monster so much he wet himself? Even though he was nine leagues high? Me.'

'I seem to recall he peed when he saw Thor, not you,' said Roskva.

'Yeah, but I killed him,' said Alfi. 'And who tricked Hrungnir and made him stand on his shield because I told him Thor would attack from below?'

'And who suggested that?' said Roskva.

'History does not relate,' said Alfi, smiling. 'Oh go on, Roskva, I know what I owe you.'

Roskva smiled a tiny smile.

'I killed a giant once,' said Snot. 'He tripped over his entrails and died.'

Uhhh. Gross. Yuck.

Freya stared at her strange companions. They were so different from her. Apart from being human, or sort of human, in Snot's case, what did they share except a terrible fate?

'Roskva . . . if you could have a wish, what would it be?' said Freya. Talking about something, anything, distracted her from brooding about the horrors which lay ahead.

'That we'd never met?' snapped Roskva.

Honestly, thought Freya. Why did she even bother talking to her?

'Roskva!' said Alfi. 'Don't mind her, Freya, she's always crabby.'

'Anyway, you have to be careful with wishes; they go wrong,' said Roskva. She grimaced.

'I used to wish for a hamster,' said Freya. 'I don't see how *that* could backfire.'

'Did your wish come true?' said Alfi.

'Nah,' said Freya. 'I got a goldfish instead.'

'A fish of gold would be a *lot* better than a hamster,' said Alfi. 'That's amazing. The Gods must hold you in high regard.'

'Oh, it wasn't *made* of gold,' said Freya. 'It was just a gold-coloured fish.' And a very dull one too: Moby

Dick had rolled on to his back and died as quickly as he could.

'I'd wish . . . I'd wish Thor had never stopped at our farmhouse,' said Roskva.

Alfi shook his head. 'I'm glad he did. Even now.'

'You're crazy,' said Roskva. 'How about you, Snot? What would you wish?'

'I'd wish to be deaf so I couldn't hear your inane babblings,' said Snot. 'Now SHUT UP!'

'From your mouth to the Gods' ears,' said Roskva, glaring at him.

Something had been niggling Freya. Something about this hall wasn't right. The shape, the side hall they were in, the four radiating halls at the end, the entrance without a door . . .

And then Freya realised where she was.

'Oh my Gods,' whispered Freya. 'This isn't a hall. It's a glove. It's a gigantic glove.'

'Uh-oh,' said Alfi. He sprang to his feet.

Roskva stayed seated.

'Well, whoever's glove it is lost it long ago,' said Roskva.

'You don't know that. What if . . . what if the giant comes back and tries to put it on?' said Freya. 'We should get out of here.' She suddenly felt like she was trapped inside a whale's belly.

'No one, not even a giant, will be looking for a lost glove in a forest at night in a storm,' said Alfi.

Roskva spread her cloak on the ground. 'I don't know about the rest of you but I'm tired,' she said. 'I'm staying here.'

After a moment's hesitation, everyone joined her.

Freya tried not to think about tomorrow. But as she lay down on the bear fur cloak, troubled thoughts whirled in her head. Even if she lived long enough to reach Thrymheim, how could Idunn still be at Thjazi's? It had all happened so long ago ... And if Idunn were still there, how could they rescue her from a giant? Freya clutched her Thor hammer charm and prayed fervently for whatever protection and luck the weary God could provide.

She was dreaming of fire. Warm, warm fire. The lovely heat, spreading through her body ... while a horse neighed and neighed ...

'Get up!' shouted Snot. 'The roof is on fire!'

The air was thick. Hot cinders fell in the darkness all around them. Freya's eyes stung and her mouth filled with acrid smoke. Her throat and nostrils burnt.

'Use Woden's charm, Snot!' screamed Roskva,

coughing. 'He gave you a fire-quenching charm! Say it! Say it!'

Snot muttered the ancient words. The fire roared louder.

Stumbling and choking, they felt their way along the bristly wall and ran outside, coughing and spluttering.

The burning glove lit up the night sky. They backed away into the forest, stumbling through the dense undergrowth, snapping rotten branches and tripping over tree roots, their sleeves and hems caught by brambly bushes.

'It didn't work, Snot!' said Roskva. 'You stupid idiot! The fire's burning harder than ever. You must have said it wrong. Say the rune again. Honestly! Do I have to do everything myself?'

She glared at Snot. Then her face softened.

'Let's get away from here,' said Alfi. 'It's not safe. Giants set that fire – they knew we were inside.'

Roskva didn't move.

'Roskva? ROSKVA!'

Roskva was blushing and gazing at Snot. But not just gazing. She was devouring him. A silly grin spread across her face and she sidled up to him, looking at him sideways with lowered lashes.

'Hello, handsome,' she said, flicking her hair and

giving him a little half-smile. 'Where have you been all my life? I never noticed before how absolutely gorgeous you are. I must have been blind.'

'What's got into you, Roskva?' said Alfi. 'We don't have time for your silliness. The whole forest is catching fire, we need to move. The giants know we're here.'

Roskva ignored him. Snot stared at her as if she'd just been changed into a salmon.

'What do you say we ditch these infants and find somewhere a little more . . . uh . . . private?' she giggled. 'To think you were in Asgard all this time and I never noticed what a handsome hunk you are.'

'Stop it, Roskva,' said Alfi. 'We're in terrible danger.'

Snot bristled.

'You making fun of me?'

Roskva's face crumpled. 'Making fun of you? Snot, I love you! I love you more than my life. You are fairer than any god. You're the sun, the moon, and the stars. None beam as brightly as your eyes. And your crooked brows . . . and strong arms . . . and muscular chest . . . and . . . and . . . Oh Gods! Let's run away together! Now! Come on! The night is young,' she simpered, tugging frantically on his hairy arm.

'It's not funny,' scowled Snot. 'Go play with the trolls.'

'It's like someone's cast a spell on her,' said Freya.

116

Grumpy, bossy, complaining Roskva was a hundred times better than this one.

Alfi slapped his forehead.

'Snot, the rune the All-Father gave you. He must have told you a love-charm instead by mistake. What are we going to do?'

'Can't you both PLEASE just go away and leave me alone with my darling love?' wailed Roskva. 'Don't you know when you're not wanted?'

'We're not going anywhere,' muttered Alfi, grabbing hold of Roskva's hand and pulling her along the path. Roskva allowed herself to be dragged for a moment, then suddenly stopped and shouted:

Oh Snot, Snot, Snot,
I feel hot hot hot
I love you a lot
My heart's tied in a knot
Some may think you're a blot
That your legs are too squat
But when I'm around you I'm besot-ot-ot-ted.

'Oh Gods, not poetry too,' said Alfi, groaning. Roskva kept trying to wind her arms around Snot's neck. Every time he peeled them off.

117

'Roskva,' said Freya. 'Please. We have a job to do . . .'

'Job!' squealed Roskva, jumping on to Snot's back. 'What job? I'm in love! I'm in love! I'm in love!'

'How long are we going to have to bear this?' said Freya.

Snot dumped Roskva, pulled out his sword and beckoned Alfi and Freya over to him.

'Stay there!' he ordered her.

'Whatever you say, my honey lamb,' she cooed.

'I say we kill her,' said Snot.

'No!' said Alfi.

'Don't you tell my darling "no" in that tone of voice,' said Roskva.

'Be calm, be calm,' said Freya. 'How long does a rune last?'

'I don't know,' said Alfi.

'Will it wear off?'

'I don't know,' said Alfi. 'Maybe. Maybe not.'

'We can tie her up and leave her to the wolves. She's useless like this,' said Snot.

'Can we reverse it?' said Freya.

'What do you mean?'

'Say the rune backwards,' said Freya.

'What and risk whipping up a storm, or causing an earthquake?' said Alfi. 'The All-Father's magic is powerful beyond all things. You don't just say these words lightly and hope for the best.'

'Got a better idea?' said Freya.

'It will never work,' said Alfi. 'Don't say the words. Don't. Don't. Please don't. She could burst into flames. She could end up hating us all. She could—'

'Oh Snotty! Where are you, my dearest darling? Don't leave me!' cooed Roskva, running over to him and covering him with kisses.

Snot gritted his teeth and recited the rune.

Roskva froze. She dropped her arms to her side and stepped back, wiping her mouth and blinking.

'Well?' she snapped. 'Why are you all looking at me? Come on, let's get out of here. We've been sleeping in a giant's glove. That's G-I-A-N-T. The fire will attract all evil creatures. What are you waiting for?'

'You,' said Alfi. He smiled at Freya.

'What's so funny?' said Roskva.

'Nothing,' said Freya.

She'd done something right. She'd actually done something right.

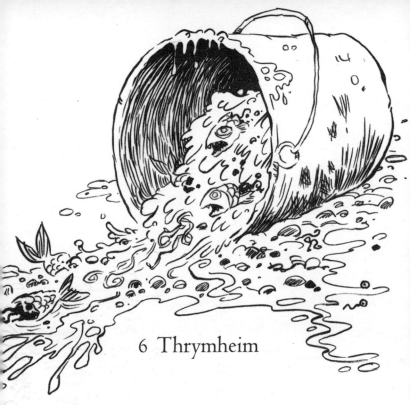

6 Thrymheim

Freya shut her eyes as Sleipnir's hooves skidded round the edge of the sheer cliff and she glimpsed the glacier-filled ravine far below. A torrential waterfall tumbled into the valley. They were now climbing steadily up the charcoal-black mountains along a treacherous track. And all the while, hail pelted them and shrill winds whipped their cloaks. Freya's breath froze and her lashes were laced with ice. Her lungs hurt every time she breathed.

Perched at the top of a high precipice loomed

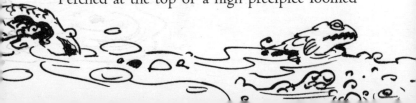

Thrymheim, Thjazi's sullen storm-home, hewn out of iron-grey rock and lashed with snow and whirling winds. It rose out of the freezing fog like a dungeon tossed above ground.

They dismounted, drenched, out of sight of the giant's lair. Freya's numb feet were soaked. Gods, she hated having wet feet. Why couldn't the Gods do their own dirty work? she thought rebelliously, slopping through the slimy snow. She staggered under the weight of Snot's sodden cloak, which hung heavy from her shoulders. She gritted her teeth. The moment she'd been dreading had arrived.

They left Sleipnir, trembling after his long climb, hidden in a dip in the rocks a short distance from the hideous hall. Freya saw his eight legs were now mottled ivory up to his great chest. She shivered, and not just from the aching cold. A few frozen sheep huddled together in a nearby stone-walled pen.

Snot led the way as they crept towards the towering lair, almost bent double in the buffeting wind. No smoke billowed from the gap at the top of the gabled roof. The gigantic front door was ajar.

'That's a stroke of luck,' said Alfi.

'It's not like he gets many visitors up here, is it?' said Roskva, raising her voice to be heard against the wind.

'But he's left the door wide open,' said Freya. She'd never do that in London. 'You don't think it's because he's . . . expecting us?'

'Let's keep watch,' whispered Roskva. 'We'll wait till he leaves, then sneak in.'

'And if he catches us?' said Freya. Her heart thudded.

'We can pretend to be servants looking for work,' said Roskva.

'Look!' hissed Alfi, pointing down.

There below the precipice, Freya glimpsed the back of a giant so huge his shoulders touched the mountains on either side of the valley as he strode away.

Freya exhaled. 'Oh my Gods,' she breathed. Even Snot paled.

'Still fancy single combat?' said Roskva.

Snot glowered and bit his battle-worn shield. 'I've never run from a fight and I won't now,' he said.

'Let's go,' said Roskva. 'Fate's given us our chance to find Idunn.'

Please Gods, prayed Freya. Please Gods let her still be here.

They crept through the door. Blustery winds gusted through the bleak, cavernous hall. Everyone shivered. Freya's teeth chattered, and her fingers were raw and icy. Had she ever been so cold before?

The wind howled, slamming doors, blowing and banging. Embers from a small fire glowed in the immense hearth by the hall's entrance, flanked by the tallest benches Freya had ever seen. The air reeked of damp decay.

They wandered in silence the length of the cold, dark, dank, filthy room, hewn from the bluish rock.

There were gigantic carved gold chairs covered in filthy blankets. Globs of greasy hair and fur clumped in corners. Moth-eaten tapestries, black with smoke, flapped in the wind. Fish guts congealed where they'd slopped on to the damp stone floor. There were cracked drinking horns, vats of ale, and barrels of stinking dried herring, along with piles of wolf pelts and bear skins. Giant nets dangled from the walls, alongside fishing poles and rusty spears. Heaps of candle wax piled up below the iron-spiked wall sconces. Bones, half-eaten, were scattered on top of bloody knives and filthy gold platters crawling with mould.

Freya felt like a little mouse scuttling about as she tried to avoid the slippery fish guts. There was junk everywhere, except the junk was all gold and silver. Thrymheim reminded her of a picture she'd once seen in *Hello!* magazine of a Russian oligarch and his spikytaloned wife enthroned in a gilded gold room. The whole place stank of fish.

And something much worse. Much, much worse. They passed reeking barrels of brown water, filled with huge floating . . . Freya recoiled, hoping it wasn't what she thought it was. The stench was unbelievable. Freya picked her way past the slops, holding her nose and retching.

There were enormous buckets crammed with fish heads up to her shoulders. One was knocked over, spilling its smelly contents on to the ground. Snot grabbed a fish head and munched. The eyeballs popped out and rolled on the floor. He swooped down and scooped them into his mouth.

'What?' he said, as Freya stared at him.

'Nothing,' she said.

They pushed open the heavy doors to the side rooms. They found two bed chambers, and a toilet so disgusting that Freya almost fainted.

'Guess he got tired of using this stinkhole,' said Roskva, holding her nose, 'so he's turned the whole place into a cesspit.'

'If he comes back let's not say we're servants looking for work,' muttered Alfi.

There was only one room left. The door was smaller

than the others, and there was a key in the lock.

Snot hoisted Roskva up on to his shoulders. Reaching as high as she could, Roskva turned the key.

The door opened. They all gasped as their eyes adjusted to the gloom.

'What a gold-hoard,' breathed Alfi.

Heaped on the floor were gleaming swords, shining shields, gold arm rings and brooches, axes with jewelled handles and ash spears inlaid with silver.

Snot pushed past him and started stuffing his knapsack with as much gold as he could scoop up. Alfi and Roskva fell upon the hoard as well, filling their pockets.

Freya hesitated. Just one of those gold arm rings or brooches must be worth . . . was it stealing, to steal from a giant? Especially a giant who had stolen Idunn?

'Stop – you're stealing . . .' began Freya.

The others ignored her. Alfi looked at her, surprised.

'This isn't stealing,' he said. 'We're plundering an enemy.'

'Doesn't your father go raiding?' said Roskva, stuffing arm rings into her pouch.

'No!' said Freya.

'How do you gain wealth then?' said Alfi.

Not by being an inner-city priestess like Clare or

working at the British museum like Bob, thought Freya. The memory of her parents bit into her heart.

'You get a job . . . and you work.'

'Like on a farm?' said Alfi. 'No one gets rich working on a farm. My parents barely had a cauldron and an oak chest. Oh, if they could see all this!'

Roskva grabbed a sword and tucked it into her belt. Then she handed Freya a long sword attached to a leather strap. 'Take this. You may need it.'

Freya stared at the sword, covered in runic inscriptions, heavy and warm in her hand. It was so leaden she could barely lift it. What would she do with a sword except trip over it? She set it back down on the heap of weapons.

'Come on, we're looking for Idunn, we don't have time to waste,' said Freya, leaving the hoard. Had the gold made them forget that almost half their bodies were now mottled ivory?

'Freya's right,' said Alfi, grabbing one last brooch as he followed her. 'We can always come back for more.'

They continued searching the entire storm-hall, every room, every chest, but there was no sign of Idunn or her apples.

'She's not here,' said Alfi, striving to be heard above the whistling wind.

'Idunn!' shouted Roskva. 'Idunn! It's Roskva. Are you here?' Her voice echoed eerily in the vast hall.

Freya felt hideously disappointed. What had she expected, to find Idunn sitting at a loom or tending to a fire? She realised she'd been hoping against hope that somehow it would all turn out right.

'Let's get some food,' said Roskva. Her teeth chattered. 'I'm starving. Then we must decide what to do.'

'Kill the giant,' snarled Snot.

Fat lot of good that will do, thought Freya.

The table was far too high to reach, so Alfi grabbed a fishing rod, scrambled up on to a bench and swept the table to knock down whatever was on it. A massive loaf of barley bread and a bowl of curds and whey flopped to the floor. They fell on the food. After the berries and the rotten oat cakes and the tree sap it tasted like heaven. Freya felt like Goldilocks. I should wash my – oh forget it, she thought, shovelling bread into her mouth. I'll be dead soon, I can live a little.

There was a fluttering sound.

'Look!' hissed Roskva. 'Oh look!' She pointed to the beam high above their heads. A mass of feathers hung over it, ruffling in the wind.

It was a falcon skin. It shimmered and glimmered,

the feathers flecked with gold and blue.

'That's Freyja's falcon skin,' said Alfi. 'I'd know it anywhere.'

'It means Loki was definitely here,' said Roskva, beaming. 'Freyja loaned it to him to fly here. He can't change into a bird: only to earth-bound creatures.'

'Then why would he leave the falcon skin behind?' said Freya.

Roskva shrugged. 'Something obviously happened to him here. There's no way he would abandon it. Maybe he left in a hurry. Maybe Thjazi killed him.'

'Maybe he froze to death,' said Alfi.

'Quick, let's get it down,' said Roskva. 'Freya can fly up to it.'

What? thought Freya. *Fly?*

The ground began to shake. There was a THUD! And then another. And another.

'Oh Gods, he's back! Hide!' said Roskva.

Snot bristled.

'I'm not hiding,' he growled. 'A berserk doesn't *hide*.'

'Shut up and hide!' ordered Roskva. 'Or we'll all die.'

Snot hesitated, then slipped into the storeroom off to the side. 'I'll kill him later,' he muttered.

The others barely had time to duck behind barrels

before a giant stomped in, carrying huge buckets of speared fish, entrails and guts.

'That's not Thjazi,' murmured Alfi. Freya could scarcely breathe. The giant was wearing a coat of mail, a battered helmet, and carried a sword and an enormous round shield emblazoned with eagles gnawing at a corpse. He took off the helmet and armour and shook out tangled frizzy green hair. Freya gasped.

It wasn't a he. It was a she. The ugliest hag Freya had ever seen, with small, squinting, bloodshot eyes and a hideous wart-covered face. Great bands of fat swelled around her middle. Her arms bulged out of her tunic sleeves. Her thighs were like tree trunks. Her short dress was far too tight. Freya had a horrible feeling she wasn't wearing any underwear.

The giantess lifted her leg and farted loudly. A terrible stink hung over the room. Freya covered her nose and tried not to breathe.

The disgusting creature picked up a vast drinking horn and gulped. She drank, and drank, and drank, the liquid pouring down her face and slopping onto the floor. She belched and wiped her dripping mouth with her sleeve.

Then she sniffed the air.

'Snugglebum? Snugglebum? Is that you?'

They froze.

The giantess continued sniffing. A huge smile gashed her face and she punched the air with her hairy fist.

'You've come back for me at last, my little snugglechops!' she cooed. 'You certainly took your time. But your itty-bitty Skadi-Waddi isn't mad. Come on out and show yourself. No need to be shy! Daddy's not at home. Just your darling Skadi!'

No one moved. Freya thought she would pass out. Thjazi had a daughter. A daughter. Now they had *two* giants to deal with.

'I can smell you, you know,' said the giantess, primping and running her thick fingers through her bristly hair. 'Why don't you come out from the storeroom and give your little Skadi a kiss? Or do I have to come and *get* you?'

Reluctantly, Roskva, Alfi, and Freya came out from behind their barrels and stood trembling at the storeroom's entrance. After a moment, Snot joined them, hand on his sword. Next to the giantess, even he looked puny as she loomed over them, glowering.

'If she attacks, use the love charm,' muttered Freya. Snot went ashen.

'I'll kill her first,' he spat.

Skadi's face fell.

'Oh,' she said. 'Oh. You're not him. You're just thieves. How dare you, you lousy, stinking—' she drew her sword. Roskva, Alfi, and Snot drew theirs.

'No!' said Alfi. 'Wait! We're not thieves. We're . . .'

'No one comes here!' bellowed Skadi, advancing towards them. 'No one. Who are you and what are you doing in my house?'

'Tell her, Roskva,' said Alfi, quaking.

Roskva glared at her brother.

'We're Thor's bondservants,' said Roskva. Her voice was shaking. 'The door was open so we came in to wait for you.'

Skadi looked confused. 'Thor's bondservants? *Thor?* Then you've come from . . . Asgard?'

Roskva nodded.

Skadi's face lit up. 'Was Loki there? Have you seen him?'

Huh?

Roskva hesitated.

'No,' said Roskva.

Skadi's face sagged. Freya held her breath. Should Roskva have lied and said yes?

'Why are you here?' roared Skadi. She glowered.

'Thor hates giants.'

Snot gripped his sword and stepped towards her.

'Back off or I'll kill you!' he bellowed.

'Use — the — charm!' hissed Freya.

'We're here . . . we're here . . .' began Roskva.

'We're here because Thor's looking for a wife,' said Freya. She had no idea how that thought popped into her head.

Skadi snorted and lowered her sword a fraction.

'He's got a wife,' said Skadi. 'That old salmon-faced Sif.'

'Not for himself,' said Roskva. 'For one of his handsome sons.'

'Which one?' said Skadi.

'Magni,' said Alfi. 'The strong one.'

'The giantess Jarnsaxa's son,' said Roskva. 'He's gorgeous.'

Skadi's eyes gleamed.

'Well, well, well. What bride gifts have you brought?'

Gifts? Gifts? They exchanged looks.

Alfi took off a gold arm band and held it out.

Skadi laughed. Her laugh was like a fox shrieking in the night.

'Is that a jest?' she said coldly. 'I don't like jests. Magni must have offered something better than a bent old bracelet to tempt me. What else?' Her voice was steel.

Freya swallowed.

Did they dare offer her one of her own gold brooches and pray Thor she wouldn't recognise it as her own? Because if she did . . .

Freya fumbled in her pocket.

'I've brought something for you, something precious and rare,' she said, taking out the KitKat and sliding it across the floor towards Skadi.

'Stay back,' ordered Skadi. 'What is it?' she asked, snatching it and sniffing the red wrapper. Her greedy eyes gleamed.

'It's called chocolate,' said Freya.

'Choc-o-late,' said Skadi, rolling the word round her mouth.

'The food of the Gods,' said Freya. 'It makes you happy.'

'How do I know it's not poisoned?' said Skadi, baring her gangrene-green teeth.

'I'll eat some,' said Freya quickly.

Skadi stuffed the entire bar into her mouth, wrapper and all.

'Delicious,' she mumbled. 'Especially the skin. What else?'

Freya reached again into her pocket. The dead mobile phone would be useless. She held out the quacking duck keyring and squeezed.

Quack!

Everyone jumped. The little light glowed.

Skadi gasped. Freya slid it towards the giantess.

'Some elf magic here . . .' murmured Skadi, marvelling at the tiny light. 'There's fire inside . . . I've never seen anything like it . . .'

Skadi squeezed the keyring. *Quack! Quack! Quack!* Everyone jumped again.

'You better –' *Quack!* – 'leave before Dad gets home. He doesn't –' *Quack!* – 'like visitors,' said Skadi. 'In fact, he usually –' *Quack!* – 'eats them.' *Quack! Quack! Quack!*

'Umm . . .' said Roskva, her eyes fixed nervously on Skadi. 'What do you think of our Master's proposal? You and Magni – is it a match?'

Skadi paused.

'You're too late,' she growled. 'I'm already betrothed.'

'Why didn't you say so before you ate my chocolate?' burst out Freya.

'Who's the lucky guy?' said Alfi.

Skadi simpered.

'Loki.'

Freya stiffened. Roskva's face didn't change.

'Oh! Great! I'm sure you'll both be very happy,' said Roskva.

'Yes,' said Skadi, sighing. 'We were made for each other.'

'So ... where's Loki now?' said Roskva carelessly. 'I'd like to congratulate him.'

Skadi glared at Roskva. Her hideous face turned green and purple.

'D'you think if I knew that I'd be standing here talking to you?' roared Skadi. Freya felt weak with fear.

Skadi began to stomp up and down the Hall, the floor shaking with every clomp.

'Where is he? Where can he be?' howled Skadi. 'I want a husband!' Her angry red eyes flashed. 'I'm sick of living with Dad and I'm certainly not getting any younger. We've eaten all the apples and—' she broke off. 'Loki said he'd marry me and make me a goddess if I gave him Idunn. We'd live half in Asgard, and half here. Obviously, when you have such a lovely home like Thrymheim you wouldn't want to leave it behind forever.'

'Obviously,' said Alfi.

'We were getting ready to run off together when Dad came home early,' said Skadi. 'Loki ran, Dad chased him, but thanks to fate Loki got away. He swore he'd come back for me as soon as he could. And I've been waiting for him ever since.'

'So he just ran off with Idunn and left you?' said Roskva. 'Typical.'

Skadi stared at her. 'What do you think I am, crazy? Of course he doesn't have Idunn. I—' Skadi brought her hand to her mouth.

'Where is she then?' said Freya.

Skadi looked at her with narrow eyes.

'None of your beeswax,' said Skadi.

Where? Where could Idunn be? They'd searched the entire storm-hall. Was there a hidden room or cellar where she was imprisoned? Had she escaped somehow?

'I've been waiting and waiting and waiting,' moaned Skadi. 'Aching with love-longing. Getting old. Getting fat. When I heard noises in the Hall I thought it was my Loki . . . at last. He'll come back. I know he will. He loves me, he's crazy about me. He says my chunky thighs and bristly chin drive him wild. He loves a warty girl. We're getting married just as soon as he returns. He swore an oath.'

'You know Loki already has a wife?' said Roskva.

Skadi grew pale.

'What?' she whispered.

'Loki has a wife,' said Roskva. 'Sigyn.'

Skadi looked as if she'd been punched in the face. She reeled back.

'You're lying,' hissed Skadi.

'Why would I lie?' said Roskva.

Skadi shook her head. 'Why would you lie? Why would you lie? A wife? A wife? What does she look like?'

'She's gorgeous,' said Roskva.

'She makes Freyja look like a shrivelled old radish,' said Alfi.

'Sif looks like a cabbage next to her,' said Roskva.

'He has a wife . . .' muttered Skadi. 'He has a wife . . . A beautiful wife. He never mentioned a wife . . . Children?'

'Two sons, Nari and Vali,' said Roskva.

Skadi groaned. 'That lying, cheating, two-faced son of an ogress . . . Loki double-crossed me. I believed him, I thought he loved me . . .' she wailed.

Freya tried to look sympathetic. She'd had a lot of practice doing that, while her parents slagged each other off.

'What a creep,' said Freya.

'He told me he would lie low in Hel, where the Gods couldn't harm him, then come back for me when it was safe. And I believed him,' said Skadi bitterly. 'I've wasted my life waiting for him.' She looked like a bloated fish gasping for breath.

'Men are awful,' said Roskva.

'Return betrayal with treachery . . . repay cunning in kind,' muttered Skadi. 'Well I'll show him . . . no one makes a fool of me.'

She reached between her enormous sagging breasts and took out a nut.

'Here,' said Skadi, holding the nut out to Freya. 'Take this and sod off before I change my mind.'

Freya flinched. She didn't want to touch anything which had been in Skadi's cleavage.

'No thanks, I'm allergic to nuts,' said Freya.

Skadi snorted. Her fetid breath reeked of rotten fish.

'Suit yourself, mortal,' she said, curling her fingers around the nut.

'Wait,' said Alfi. He went pale.

'Is that – Idunn?' said Roskva.

Skadi smiled, flashing her fangs.

'Loki changed her into a nut,' said Skadi. 'Give this to Magni as a wedding gift. I accept the proposal.'

Freya gazed open-mouthed. She couldn't move. She couldn't breathe. How stupid she was! She could scarcely believe it. Everyone crowded round and gazed at the small brown nut clutched in Skadi's leathery hand.

'Go on, take her!' screamed Skadi, hurling the nut against the wall. 'Serve Loki right. Betrayal must be repaid with treachery.'

Freya lunged and grabbed the precious nut as it bounced off the wall and rolled across the floor. It felt warm and smooth in her trembling hand. She held it tightly. They had found Idunn! Now all they had to do was race to Asgard and they'd be free.

'GO!' screamed Skadi. 'My father will be back any moment. If he finds you here he'll dash your brains out on the stones and let the wolves in to lap them up.'

Skadi picked up a stool and hurled it against the wall. It splintered. Freya ducked. Her mother hurled plates sometimes, but . . .

'That dirty rotten scoundrel!' bellowed Skadi, hurling a chair.

CRASH.

'That filthy son of a mare!'

SMASH.

'May his body be flayed by fire!'

CRASH. SMASH.

'May he be bound with his son's guts and poison splashed on his face!'

SPLINTER.

'I'll twist his head from his miserable body, that herring-faced manure-breath troll fart! I won't be made a fool of! I'll rip his body to pieces and give them to the trolls to eat!'

The hall quaked as she screamed and rampaged, cursing and stomping and bellowing.

'Let's get out of here,' said Alfi. 'She could change her mind any moment.'

The four fled outside into the hail. Freya barely noticed the frosty winds lashing them. The relief she felt was indescribable. By some incredible, unexpected whim of fate, they had succeeded in their impossible quest. If the fates continued to smile on them, the Gods would be restored to life and youth, and Freya could return home and this would all be some terrible nightmare which had happened in another time and another life and another world. She prayed to Thor to keep Thjazi well away from them until they were safely back in Asgard.

They ran to Sleipnir. The grey horse reared, pawing the sky. Icicles clung to his mane, which rattled and clinked as he shook his great head. His breath looked ghostly in the frosty air.

'We've got her!' Roskva rejoiced. Her plain, angry

face had lost its fretful expression. 'I don't know how, but . . . we got Idunn!'

Even Snot smiled.

Alfi did a little dance.

'Yes!' he said, smiling. 'Or is it, woo hoo! Now let's run from this horrible place before Thjazi gets back and finds Idunn missing.'

Alfi scrambled up on to Sleipnir's back, then leaned down to help Freya mount. Snot linked his ivory-laced hands to give her something to step on to.

One moment Freya had her hand on Sleipnir's neck, the next he'd vanished. Freya's wrist was caught in a man's tight grip. A handsome man with one green eye, one red.

'I'll have that, thanks!' he roared, snatching the nut from her and pushing her hard. Freya glimpsed his mottled ivory hand as she reeled and fell over.

'See you in Hel!' he jeered.

Then he murmured something and changed back into the eight-legged horse, kicked Snot away, then galloped off riderless down the sloping path from Thrymheim. Roskva lunged for the reins but Sleipnir was too fast and she fell. In a moment he was gone.

Alfi lay stunned on the icy ground, sprawled

beneath Snot, who was grunting and clutching his hip where Sleipnir had kicked him.

Freya looked down at her empty ivory hand. What had just happened? Who was that man?

'Loki,' moaned Roskva.

7 Hekla

Loki.

'The Wolf's father,' gasped Alfi. 'He was here . . .'

'I don't understand,' said Freya. The others stared shell-shocked where Sleipnir had been tethered. Roskva opened her mouth and then closed it. Her shoulders slumped.

'Will someone please tell me what just happened!' screamed Freya. She kept looking at her shaking hand, which had held Idunn for such a brief moment. 'I had her, I had her . . .' she wailed.

'Shut up!' raged Snot. 'Just shut up!' He clamped

his hand across her mouth. Freya flailed at him and he released her, roaring like a mad animal.

'Somehow Loki slipped into the sleeping army disguised as Sleipnir,' said Roskva tonelessly. Her face was ashen.

'But *how*? How?'

'He's a shape-shifter,' said Alfi. His voice was bitter. 'He's a liar, and the father of monsters.'

'And he's been hiding with us the whole time . . .' said Freya. She was having trouble taking this in.

'If I'd known I would have torn out his throat,' snarled Snot. He was limping badly. Blood stained his bear-skin tunic and dripped down his leg.

'We should have guessed he'd find a way to live while the Gods were dying,' said Roskva. Angrily, she brushed away tears. 'Fate chose us for misfortune.'

Freya felt numb. She could still feel Loki's fingers on her shoulders where he'd shoved her. All around her the wind howled, and the world was as desolate as her spirits.

'Oh Gods, we were so close . . . so close . . .' said Roskva, scrambling to her feet.

'We have to get away,' said Alfi. 'Then we'll decide what to do.'

There was nothing to do, thought Freya. They'd lost.

How they got down from Thrymheim into the valley below Freya never knew. She skidded down the icy path, stumbling, falling over, Roskva and Alfi urging her to move faster, Snot limping and cursing and raging as she clung to him for balance. The closer the rocky trail got to the waterfall, the mossier and slippier it became.

'All isn't lost,' said Alfi, clenching his fists. 'We just have to find Loki and get Idunn back.'

Freya stared at him. 'Just?' she said.

Alfi might as well have said 'We just have to turn into dinosaurs and jump to the moon.'

'And how are we going to find him?' said Roskva. 'Loki could be anywhere in the nine worlds.' She pushed up her long linen sleeve. The mottled ivory was nearing her elbow.

'We're doomed,' said Snot. 'It's over.' A trickle of blood ran from his ripped tunic. 'We should find somewhere dry and wait till our fate summons us.'

There was a silence. Freya listened to the waterfall as it pounded into the rocks, shielding her face from the biting sleet. To sit and rest, just to accept fate . . .

So much for Woden's charms and runes and wisdom. The Trickster had defeated them. Her last meal would be gruel, then she would learn to say toilet in twenty-six languages as she stood frozen for eternity as a chess piece in the British Museum. She'd never see her parents or her friends again. Silent tears trickled down her face. She'd always known their quest was hopeless.

'Wait,' said Roskva. 'Wait. What did Loki say when he snatched Idunn?'

Who cares what he said?

'He said, "See you in Hel,"' muttered Freya.

'Why did he say that?' said Roskva.

'Because we're all going to die,' said Alfi.

'No-o,' said Roskva. 'No. He was taunting us. That's where he's gone . . .'

Alfi gasped. He stopped so abruptly the others all bumped into him.

'Hel? He's gone to Hel?'

'The Realm of the Dead?' said Freya.

'What makes you so sure?' said Alfi.

'It's where he told Skadi he would hide from the Gods,' said Roskva. 'They have no power there. Hel is his daughter and she alone rules that grim world named for her. Loki can wait in Hel until the Gods die then he'll be free to do as he likes.'

'But why hide? He's got Idunn now,' said Freya.

'That doesn't matter,' said Roskva. Her face lit up.

'You saw his ivory hand. He's like us. Idunn can keep him young but he'll still turn back into a chess piece if we don't restore Idunn to the Gods. Hel is the only place he can go where Woden's charm can't affect him.'

'Unless Loki's taken Idunn back to Asgard like he promised,' said Alfi.

'You think he has?' said Roskva.

'No,' said Alfi. 'That's not Loki's nature.'

'The apples of Hel,' murmured Freya. 'We had to learn a poem in school once about them.'

'Meaning?' said Roskva.

'Well,' said Freya, 'the poem makes a bit more sense if Loki actually took Idunn's apples there . . . oh, never mind,' she said.

'If Loki's gone to Hel then we have to follow him,' said Alfi. His bulging eyes were very wide. 'Going to Hel . . .' He shook his head in disbelief.

'That means finding Helveg,' said Roskva. 'There's no other way there.'

'Helveg?' said Freya apprehensively.

'The dark road to Hel,' said Alfi. 'No light touches it.'

Roskva suddenly gasped and shook her head.

They conferred rapidly in their own language, gesticulating and shouting.

'What are you saying?' said Freya. 'Please speak so I can understand.'

Roskva grimaced. All the happiness had drained from her face.

'I told him the truth: Hel is too far away. Riding Sleipnir was our only chance,' said Roskva. 'On foot we'll never get there in time.' She peered down her tunic. 'My body is more than half ivory now,' she said. 'We have . . . what? Four nights left? We'll be chess pieces again long before we ever reach the entrance and Hel's dog eats us.'

'I can run,' said Alfi stubbornly.

'Even you're no match for Sleipnir. Helveg is many nights' travel from here. It's much further than Asgard.' She sighed. The wind swirled round her cloak.

'So that's why Loki told us where he was going,' said Alfi.

'He was gloating. He knows we have no chance of reaching Hel before our time is up.'

'So we're stuffed?' said Freya.

'Stuffed?'

'Finished. It's over. We're history,' said Freya. All that effort and cold and wet and terror – for nothing. She felt more tired than she had ever felt in her life.

'There is another way to Hel,' said Snot.

The others stared at him.

'What other way?' said Alfi. 'Helveg is the only road.'

'Hekla,' said Snot.

There was total silence. Alfi and Roskva looked at one another.

'Are you crazy?' said Alfi.

'What's Hekla?' said Freya. The word had an ugly cackling sound. It didn't sound good.

'Hekla is a volcano and entrance to Hel,' said Alfi. 'No one goes anywhere near there.'

Freya closed her eyes. Oh Gods!

'I can't climb down a volcano,' said Freya. She couldn't even make it up and down the climbing wall at the local sports centre. 'You'll have to go without me.'

'Who said anything about climbing down, stupid?' said Roskva. 'Remember the All-Father's gift?'

The falcon skin. Freya felt the quivering feather in her pocket. She'd forgotten all about it.

Why oh why hadn't Woden given the falcon skin to one of the others? She was supposed to *fly* down a volcano?

'Wait. What about you?' said Freya. Cold sweat started to collect in her armpits.

'What about us?' said Roskva. She avoided catching Freya's eye.

'How will you . . . oh I see. You won't. Just me. I'll be going to Hel alone. I'll be jumping into a volcano alone.' Freya thought she would faint.

'Look on the bright side,' said Alfi. 'This way you won't have to get past Hel's dog Garm. He's chained in the cliff cave by the road entrance.'

'Big whoop,' said Freya. She felt hysterical.

'Big whoop?' said Alfi.

'Forget it,' said Freya. This wasn't happening.

'Snot, can you guide us to Hekla?' said Roskva.

Snot nodded. 'My father's farm—'

There was a deafening roar behind them. The ground shook as if an earthquake had struck.

'WHERE IS SHE? GIVE HER BACK! THIEVES! THIEVES!' thundered a voice from above. The bellow rang round the mountains and echoed back across the valley and the sky.

'This way!' said Snot, heading straight for the waterfall. They edged their way along a narrow, rocky ledge running behind the torrential fall, clinging to the slimy rocks, trying not to tumble on to the sharp boulders below.

'GIVE HER BACK!'

Freya huddled with the others, panting, hiding behind the curtain of cascading water which tumbled over the precipice and frothed into an iceberg-filled lagoon. They pressed flat against the wet rocks, listening to the pounding footsteps stampeding towards them.

Freya caught a glimpse of Skadi's hideous legs crashing through the water. The legs stopped. Freya could feel Skadi listening. Everyone held their breath. Then suddenly the legs continued splashing through the deep water as Skadi shambled into the valley.

'Let every evil being have you,' muttered Alfi.

'And your father,' added Roskva.

They waited until the ground stopped shaking, then hurried off in the opposite direction, hugging the cliffs.

'I think we've tricked her,' murmured Roskva.

'Or she's gone to warn Thjazi . . .' said Alfi. Anxiously, they scanned the oppressive sky for any sign of the giant eagle.

'Let's find a place to cross and put the river between us and her,' said Roskva.

'Follow me!' said Alfi. 'I remember a good spot where the river is low.'

They jumped from the rocks and ran as fast as they

could along the reedy bank. The waterfall tumbled over black boulders, pouring downstream. Gradually, the angry current slowed as they rounded the bend, the river widened and the land flattened. The water streaming over the worn rocks, though still fast-flowing, looked no higher than Freya's ankles.

'Here,' said Alfi. 'It gets deeper again further on.'

Snot knelt by the water's edge, peeled the corner of his tunic off his hairy body where it was stuck with dried blood, and grimaced at the hoof-shaped gash in his mottled-ivory flesh.

'Are you hurt?' said Freya.

'It's nothing,' he snapped, splashing the icy water on the wound. 'Move!'

The four picked their way across the rocks jutting out of the shallow riverbed. Alfi, sure-footed as a goat, held Freya's hand to steady her on the slippery stones as he leapt from one to another. Freya shivered and gasped as the freezing water crept up to her calves. As they neared the middle of the river, the water suddenly deepened. She gave up trying to keep her skirt dry. Her teeth chattered. The river appeared to be rising fast. Many of the rocks were now hidden beneath the churning torrent.

'Why is this current flowing faster?' said Roskva,

as the bubbling river lapped above her waist. 'And it's getting warmer.'

'I don't like this,' said Snot, now wading up to his knees. 'Hurry.'

They picked their way across, stumbling, as the water rose higher and higher above their waists.

'She's changed her mind!' yelled Roskva.

Freya looked upstream and saw Skadi straddling the river. A gush of water poured from her.

'Oh Gods, she's *peeing* in the river!' screamed Alfi.

'I'll kill her!' howled Snot. 'I hope she goes where the trolls get her.'

The frothing yellowish water rose above Freya's shoulders. The stream had become a raging torrent. Suddenly it was above their heads and they were swept off their feet and whirled downstream, tumbling towards a precipice.

'Roskva!' gurgled Alfi. 'Use the wave-calming rune!'

Roskva babbled the ancient words the All-Father had given her. On the river bank a mound of earth began to stir as the surging river broke again over Freya's head and pulled her beneath. Freya tried to undo the heavy bear cloak weighing her down but her fingers were too numb. The river dragged her deeper and she was drowning in a whirlpool of water. She struggled and fought but her clothes were too heavy and the current too strong.

And then suddenly she wasn't being swept downstream any more but spinning in one place like a mad bug.

Thank Woden his charm had worked.

Coughing and spluttering, Freya fought her way to the surface. Her feet scrabbled to get a hold and she grabbed onto a small tree growing out of the riverbed, on which her cloak had tangled.

'Hold on!' yelled Snot, clinging to an overhanging branch.

Freya managed to brace her feet against the tree and she swung herself away from the current's force into the shallower depth. She coughed and spluttered and gulped great mouthfuls of air.

Snot grabbed Roskva's cloak as the flood-waters swept her past, yanking her to safety. Alfi landed hard against a boulder. The river, far from subsiding, looked as wild as ever.

'The charm?' spluttered Freya. 'What's happened?'

'The bloody thing didn't work,' said Roskva, coughing and gasping. 'The rowan tree saved us.'

They clung to the branches, panting and shaking and catching their breath. Then they stumbled, dripping and muddy, through the shallows towards the far side.

A pale spectre rose out of the oozing grave mound amidst the reeds and rushes, and hovered, glaring at them.

'Who forces me up?' she moaned.

Alfi, Roskva, Freya and Snot looked at one another and froze.

'Not us,' said Roskva.

'Look here, I've been dead a long time,' said the spectre. 'Someone made me appear. You think I'd just pop out of my comfy mound for my own amusement? Think again, daughter of a pig.'

Roskva shook the river water and giant pee out of her hair.

'How dare you insult me?'

The gleaming spectre laughed.

'I can insult who I like. Snow has fallen on me, rain has pelted me, I have been dead a long while. What are you going to do, kill me?'

'I think the All-Father got his runes muddled again,' muttered Alfi.

Was this the spirit version of a wrong number? thought Freya.

'For the last time, why are you bothering me?' hissed

the spectre, fizzing and steaming.

'We didn't mean to—' spluttered Alfi.

'Since you're here,' said Roskva, 'what is our fate? Will we recover Idunn? Seeress! You must answer my question.'

'I'm not a seeress, you disgusting dishrag,' raged the spectre. 'Just a dead person minding her own business in her own burial mound. If only I'd brought my axe . . .'

'Then tell us about Hel,' said Roskva. 'Has Loki been there? You must answer my question. I've summoned you in Woden's name.'

The spectre fluttered.

'What do you mean, must? Who wants to know?'

'Roskva, Thor's bondservant,' said Roskva.

'Oh him,' sneered the spectre. 'That old blustering lump. And I had that Woden summoning me long ago; he pretended to be Vegtam the Wanderer. I saw through that old magician instantly.'

'Seeress,' said Alfi, 'what wisdom can you give us? Please tell us about Hel.'

'You'll find out soon enough, looking at the state of you,' said the spectre. 'I will say no more. Okay, I'll tell you one thing. Watch out for the corpse-eating dragon Nidhogg. He eats everything that moves . . . and everything that doesn't. He likes trading insults with the eagle who lives on top of Yggdrasil. The squirrel Ratatosk carries messages between them.'

That was the wisdom? thought Freya. Useless. Useless. Useless.

'Please,' said Freya, gritting her teeth. 'Was Loki there?'

'I've told you quite enough already,' said the spectre, starting to dissolve into the earth.

'You've told us nothing! Is Loki there now?' said Freya. 'Is he on his way?'

'That's for me to know and you to find out,' said the seeress, sinking back into her weed-covered grave mound.

'Gods, I'd like to give her a good kick,' said Roskva. 'In fact, I will,' she said, marching up to the ancient barrow and kicking it as hard as she could.

Freya wished like anything she was brave enough to do the same. She half-expected the wraith to rise again, wielding her axe, but the grave mound remained still.

'You'd think the old grump would be grateful for a bit of conversation,' said Alfi, shaking his head.

They scrambled past the spectre's hill home and wrung the filthy water from their wet clothes. Freya's feet squelched. I'll never ever get dry and clean again, she mourned. But she was grateful she still had her shoes – Roskva had lost a boot.

She quickly wound a piece of cloth around her foot instead. 'It doesn't matter – what do you think I wore on my feet before Thor took us?' Roskva said. 'Boots are for the wealthy.'

Far off in the distance, high in the mist, Freya saw a black speck flying across the sun. The speck turned into a giant eagle circling and swooping frantically above the waterfall. She gasped and pointed.

They raced for cover to a thicket of trees and dived under a mass of ferns beneath a rotten tree trunk. A huge black shadow blotted out the sun and passed above the river as the eagle continued its search.

'That disgusting son of a mare! Gods, I hate giants,' growled Snot.

'He thinks we still have Idunn,' whispered Alfi. 'And when he doesn't find our bodies downstream he'll hunt us everywhere.'

Roskva was breathing hard and struggling to catch her breath. 'If we cut north through the forest and keep to the shadows we may escape him. He'll look for us on the road to Asgard. He won't know we're heading for Hekla.'

'He won't give up until he finds Idunn,' said Alfi.

'We have to make sure we find her first,' said Freya.

'The hornblower joins us at last,' said Roskva. Freya looked at her, but there was no anger in her weary, dirt-streaked face.

'There's something else,' said Roskva. She hesitated. 'We should separate. Someone needs to get to Asgard and tell the All-Father what's happened, in case . . .'

Freya thought her heart would stop. They couldn't just . . . just . . . leave her . . .

'I can't find Hekla on my own!' squeaked Freya. First they want her to fly into a volcano, then they just abandon her . . .

'Not you,' snapped Roskva. 'Alfi or me.'

'The All-Father told us to stay together,' said Freya.

'And he also told us to calm waves with a charm to raise the dead,' said Roskva. 'He's not all there any more. If I could think of another way believe me I would.'

'I'll go,' said Alfi.

'No!' said Freya.

'I'll go,' said Snot.

Much better, thought Freya.

Alfi shook his head.

'Snot must stay and get Freya to Hekla. I'm fast. If I'm travelling alone I can reach Asgard in four nights. I'll be able to talk to the All-Father before I turn back into . . . that is, if Freya doesn't . . .' He didn't finish.

The brother and sister looked at one another and nodded.

'Alfi,' said Roskva. 'Wait. Travel under cover of darkness. Keep out of the eagle's sight for as long as you can.'

'Duh,' said Alfi.

'I wish you wouldn't do that,' said Roskva. 'It's so annoying when you try to talk like her.'

'I never say duh,' said Freya.

They stood awkwardly, in silence. Alfi kicked away some dead leaves. Freya watched her breath steam in the frosty air. The wintry forest surrounding them seemed vast and lonely.

'Wait, Alfi, I have an idea,' said Freya. 'If Thjazi sees you, Gods forbid, throw a nut as far away from you as you can – he'll think it's Idunn and that'll give you time to escape.'

'Good thinking,' said Roskva. She sounded surprised. 'We should all keep nuts in our hands just in case. Good thinking . . .'

'I'm not a total idiot,' said Freya.

'Something else,' said Roskva. She seemed reluctant to let Alfi go. 'Remember—'

There was a crashing through the undergrowth and

162

a hideous troll lurched out of the trees and blocked their path.

'These are *my* woods,' he growled, fixing them with his small, greedy eyes. 'No one crosses through them without my consent. I challenge you to a contest: who can name the Gods and the elves one by one. The winner will eat the loser,' he added, slobbering.

Alfi's face lit up. He muttered something under his breath and stepped forward.

Oh no, thought Freya. What happens now? Will witches be knocked off rafters? Will hanged men start speaking? Will shackles spring open?

'I accept your challenge,' said Alfi. 'I'll start. Aldafodr.'

'Arnhofdi,' spat the troll.

'Audun,' said Alfi.

'Bragi,' said the troll.

'Draugadrottin,' said Alfi.

'Einibr—'

An axe whirred through the air and landed in the troll's head. The monster fell backwards, dead.

'We don't have time for this,' said Snot, retrieving his bloody weapon.

'But the All-Father's charm actually worked,' said Alfi. 'I knew—'

'Go!' said Snot. 'Go to Asgard! Before I throw something at *you*.'

'Alfi,' said Roskva. 'Be careful. Please.'

Alfi ran. One moment he was there amidst the fir trees, the next he was a blur.

Freya glanced at Roskva. She turned away but not before Freya saw that her eyes were filled with tears.

'He's all that's left,' said Roskva. 'We've always been alone in Asgard. Who else could understand our strange life – two mortals who live with the Gods?'

They hid until dusk, then travelled almost without stop, in a tense, desperate silence. That night there was a bright full moon, so they criss-crossed through the grim woods for as long as they could see the narrow path, sleeping at dawn for a few short hours anywhere that was dry and hidden until the sky darkened again and they felt safer from the eagle's prowling gaze.

For three days and nights they travelled. This time there was no talk, no poetry. They grabbed blackberries and blueberries, ate roots and nuts, drank water from the little streams which bubbled up. As they hurried through the bleak forests of fir and beech, silent, exhausted, frightened, Freya felt like she was marching to her death.

Once they found a hidden hot spring bubbling up in a crevasse and bathed quickly, the others keeping an eye on the sky. Freya never wanted to get out. Until she looked down at her scratched body, and flinched. The ivory tendrils were now reaching towards her neck. Soon they would be strangling her. She jumped out of the water, drying herself with her filthy clothes.

Putting them back on again was horrible.

They walked and walked and walked. Freya's feet were raw and blistered, her legs covered in scratches and bruises. She was glad she couldn't see her face.

Her world had shrunk: wet; tired; trees; blisters; scared. And then even smaller: Tired. Scared. And then she was too tired to be scared. Had her life ever been otherwise?

I can't do this, she thought. I can't go on. She trudged, one foot in front of the other. One step. And another. And another. Every step, she reminded herself, was one she would never have to take again. She was tangled in a maze of trees without end. And always constantly checking the sky, for Thjazi and his talons.

She remembered a French marching song about a hen who kept losing her chicks, which Bob had taught her for their holiday in Normandy, when she was very little and refused to go on walks.

She sang the song under her breath, and when the hen had lost all thirty of her chicks, Freya started again. Roskva joined in.

'What happens if we – if we're too late?' said Freya. She couldn't bring herself to say 'fail'. 'And we turn back into—'

Roskva trembled. 'You hear and don't hear. You see and don't see. It's like being a rock. Or a tree. Gradually, you stop knowing. Or caring. You're alone. Alone with all the other rocks and trees . . . Can we not talk about it,' said Roskva. 'You'll find out soon enough.'

Freya held out her hand, and Roskva took it.

Slowly, gradually, the forest thinned, and the path became more like a track, strewn with loose stones. They crossed cooled lava beds, twisted ropes of sharp, grey rocks edged with white, jutting up amidst acid-green mosses. Freya felt like she was walking on needles. And always, getting closer and closer to the dark volcano ridges looming above them in the first faint rays of dawn light.

The land began to smoke. Tiny pools of brownish, murky water hissed and seethed. Freya bent down and felt the earth. It was warm.

Snot gazed at the barren lava field covering the

narrow valley. 'My father's farm was here,' he said. 'Long ago.'

'I'm sorry,' said Freya.

Snot shrugged. 'Bloody stupid place to have a farm, below a volcano, if you ask me. But no one did . . .'

Freya stared up at the ominous, cratered ridges, some dotted with snow and shrouded by clouds. Thin plumes of steam curled from the tops.

Snot scanned the pinkish sky, sword drawn. His neck was starting to turn ivory. 'We can't wait until nightfall,' said Snot. 'We'll have to risk climbing Hekla in daylight.'

'Should I fly up?' said Freya. It was the last thing she wanted to say but the words came out of her mouth before she could stop them.

'It's too dangerous to fly – if Thjazi spots you he'll kill you easily in the sky,' said Roskva.

'We can protect you better on foot,' said Snot. 'We'll walk up Hekla.'

Freya was secretly relieved. Exhausted as she was, blistered and sore though her feet were, the thought of flying terrified her. She gazed up at the iron-dark mountains. Fire and smoke and ash spewed high into the air.

'Umm,' said Freya. 'We're walking up a volcano,

right? What if it erupts?'

'Then that will be how fate has decreed we die,' said Roskva.

They hastened up the volcano's dark face, sulphurous steam whistling out of fissures in the jagged rocks. On and on, up and up they climbed, crunching bits of ice underfoot, until the sun was high in the sky. A nearby volcano puffed, and then orange-red fire spewed from its molten mouth. Freya coughed and spluttered as she walked through rivers of billowing smoke.

Suddenly the air filled with ash. Chunks of ice and fire hurtled high into the sky. Steam swaddled them. From the plateau they stood on, she could see lava flowing, thick and molten and gloopy. Ice and steam, hot and cold. Surveying the burnt landscape, Freya felt she was already in the Underworld.

'Don't tell me — that's Hekla,' she moaned, as a nearby volcano belched a fresh shower of fire and lava. 'I'll die the moment I enter it . . .'

'No,' said Snot. 'We're standing on Hekla.'

Freya felt her heart stop.

'So soon?' said Freya. During the long walk up to the peak, she'd tried not to think about the horror awaiting her.

Freya gulped. Hekla's mouth opened out of the

rock, a yawning black cavern waiting to swallow her. Shaking, she crept to the rim and peered in. It was like looking into Mordor.

'No one has ever dared come up here before,' said Snot. 'We're the first.' Freya noticed he stood well back, as if he might get sucked into the world beneath the worlds.

They stood awkwardly, watching wisps of steam curl up from Hekla's grisly mouth.

'Get on with it,' said Snot, glancing nervously at the sky, sword drawn.

How could there be a blue sky, as if all was well in the world, when everything was so wrong?

Trembling, Freya took out the gleaming falcon feather and shook it. The grey-white blue-flecked feather glimmered and fluttered and took bird-shape. She spread out the falcon skin and held it in her shaking hands. The others gathered around her. Freya felt like a sacrifice to some implacable god.

She swallowed and peeked again into Hekla's black depths. How do I know it won't erupt? she thought, shuddering.

'I'll stand guard,' said Snot. He gripped his heavy sword. 'If Thjazi comes I'll be ready for him.'

'Don't be stupid, Snot,' snapped Roskva. Her voice

was shaking. 'We can't wait up here. We might as well hang out a sign with an arrow saying, "Come and get us, Thjazi!" We're visible for miles.'

'Roskva's right,' said Freya. Ugh, how she hated saying that.

'If death ambushes us, you must fly straight back to Asgard,' said Roskva. 'Can you find your way?'

Freya felt like crying.

'I don't know,' said Freya. Her mouth was dry and she could barely speak. Compared to what lay ahead, getting to Asgard seemed the least of her woes. 'Where is it?' she asked through her tears.

Roskva pointed. 'Do you see those black mountains? They're the mountains of Jotunheim. Asgard lies behind them. Head straight for those mountains then veer north and upwards. You'll see the world tree Yggdrasil rising high into the heavens . . . really, you can't miss it.'

Don't bet on that, thought Freya. She had no sense of direction at all. She could get lost going to the loo and back. One mountain looked like any other to her. And which way was north?

Freya stared at the falcon skin in her hands. She felt absolutely frozen, unable to move. Roskva spoke to her, and it was as if she were already far, far away.

'. . . and *try* not to get your blood sucked out by Nidhogg.'

'Nidhogg?' said Freya. Her head was spinning.

'The corpse-eating dragon the spectre warned you about,' said Roskva. 'Do your best to distract him.'

'Thanks for sharing, Roskva,' said Freya. She held out the falcon skin, the feathers fluttering. 'If you think I'm so useless you're welcome to fly down to see Hel yourself.'

Roskva glared at her. 'The All-Father gave *you* the falcon skin, not me,' she said. 'Only you can do this. Unfortunately.'

A horrible image came to Freya. If fate decreed she get out alive, let alone with Idunn, Thjazi would be searching the skies waiting to tear her apart. She saw herself ripped to pieces by the giant eagle, the nut falling from her grasp . . .

'I can't do this!' wailed Freya. 'Any of this!'

'We all have to do things we can't do,' said Roskva. 'Freya? Put on the falcon skin! Now. It's time.' She lifted her head, and Freya glimpsed her mottled ivory neck.

Freya's hand trembled, then she flung the gleaming falcon skin over her shoulders.

Instantly Freya's flesh prickled as feathers burst

forth and her body shuddered and twisted as her bones shrank and bent.

One moment she was a girl. The next she was a falcon.

How do I change back? thought Freya frantically, tottering on her little stick legs. I forgot to ask the Gods. How will I get out of Hel? I'm alive. Will I be stuck there forever?

'I wish we could come with you,' said Roskva suddenly.

Freya opened her beak. Then she swivelled her head as her newly keen eye glimpsed a dark shape bearing down on them across the empty sky. She squawked.

The others turned and saw the gigantic eagle approaching, talons outstretched.

'Go! Go!!' shrieked Roskva, drawing her sword. Snot raised his and they turned to face the dive-bombing 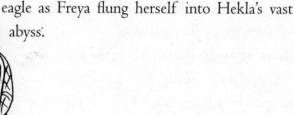 eagle as Freya flung herself into Hekla's vast abyss.

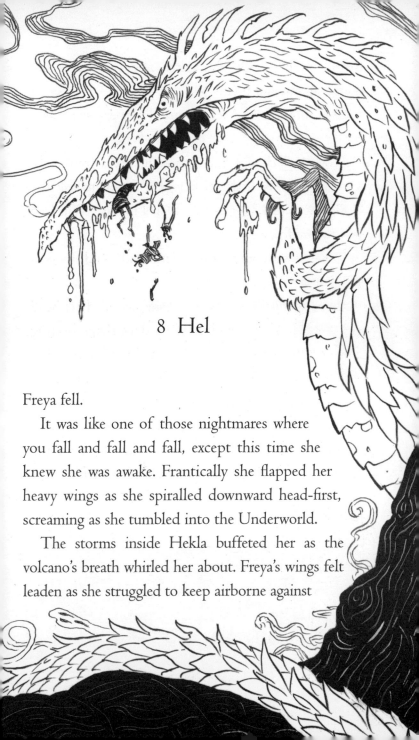

8 Hel

Freya fell.

It was like one of those nightmares where you fall and fall and fall, except this time she knew she was awake. Frantically she flapped her heavy wings as she spiralled downward head-first, screaming as she tumbled into the Underworld.

The storms inside Hekla buffeted her as the volcano's breath whirled her about. Freya's wings felt leaden as she struggled to keep airborne against the winds flinging her against the volcano's jagged sides. Freya could feel icy fingers reaching for her as she plummeted.

Were the others alive? Was Thjazi pursuing her even now?

One moment she thought she would die of heat, and prayed that Hekla wasn't about to explode. Then icy blasts bit through her feathered body and a shroud of frost enveloped her as she was yanked ever-deeper into the darkness.

Desperately she tried to right herself as she was swirled about. She had no idea if she was right side up and which way she was facing as she was twisted and twirled. Her stomach heaved.

Then, gradually, she found a way to spread her wings into the volcano's gusts, and began to glide downwards less violently.

Freya had no idea how long she spiralled in her swooping fall. The yawning steep widened and widened and widened and then – THUD! THUNK! She collided with the earth.

Freya tumbled and rolled and came to a halt, wings outstretched.

She had stopped falling.

Freya lay on the cold ground, so dizzy and battered

it was hard for her to imagine ever moving again. But she was alive — at least she thought she was alive — in the frozen gloom of the Underworld.

Freya shook herself, and the falcon skin slid off her back as easily as if she'd undone Snot's cloak. Instantly her bruised body uncurled and stretched and re-filled her skin as she regained human form. She groped around in the dark for the precious feather, found it, and put it inside her pocket.

Slowly, shakily, she raised herself on to her knees. Her arms ached. She became aware of the sound of water flowing nearby.

She had fallen beside a vast, bubbling lake, reeking sulphur, punctured with boulders. Great geysers of lava and flame leapt from the oily surface. And yet Freya saw her breath, chill and frosty, in the murky black.

As her eyes adjusted to the gloom, she saw that the flashes of light came from a glittering, gold-covered bridge. Frost rose from the river flowing beneath, lumpen with knobbly blocks of ice.

Freya watched as the shadowy blurs of corpses streamed soundlessly across the Echoing Bridge. On the other side stood a pale young giantess, watching silently as the dead flitted past.

Maybe I can blend in with them, thought Freya.

She tip-toed across the bridge, barely able to see in front of her through the mist and the hastening shades. Despite her efforts to walk quietly, her footsteps echoed as loudly as if an army were stomping by. Glints of gold from the bridge's sides flashed in the darkness. Freya felt the freezing waters beckoning her to hurl herself over the edge.

'Hey you! Stomping across like that. Are you trying to wake the dead? Yes, you!' came a shout as the girl held up her pale arm and blocked Freya's path. 'You're not dead! Who in Hel's name are you and what do you think you're doing here?'

'I'm Freya, and I've been sent from Asgard,' said Freya. She stared at the young giantess, white as chalk.

'Pull the other one,' said the giantess.

'It's true,' said Freya. 'You think I wanted to come here?'

'No one wants to come here,' said the guardian. 'But here is where everyone ends up.'

'I've come to find Loki,' said Freya. 'Has he passed by?'

The girl snorted.

'He comes and goes as he pleases,' she said.

'And has he pleased recently?'

The girl shrugged. 'Dunno.'

'Wait,' said Freya. 'Did Sleipnir pass this way?'

The girl smiled. 'Woden's riderless horse galloped over this bridge not so long ago,' she said.

So Roskva was right.

'He'll have gone to Hel's hall,' said the young guardian of the bridge. 'It's much further down. Past the shore of corpses and the Carrion-Gate.'

Freya shuddered at the hideous names.

The giantess pointed to the bleak road, then stood aside to let Freya pass.

Freya walked through the mist, straining to see, and shivering as the dripping vapour enveloped her. Shards of ice gave off tiny pinpricks of light. She could barely breathe in the horrible smell of Hel's ghastly and rotting fog-world. The place was as dreadful as the worst of fears. It was like being sucked into a grave mound, knowing you would never, ever escape.

The road dropped deeper, running alongside a hissing river, bubbles belching out of the boiling mud. The shades of the dead stretched out to her as she hurried towards the mournful citadel rising high and impregnable before her. There was a bump-bump-bump sound as chunks of ice hurtled against the river bank. Freya recoiled.

What she had thought were blocks of ice were bodies. The icy river was choked with carcasses, all being whirled downwards towards their grisly fate on the shore of corpses.

Freya whimpered and squeezed her eyes tight shut. She breathed deeply. I must go on, she thought. I must go on.

Then she heard an odd crunching sound. Freya peered through the dismal light. A red eye glowered at her.

The dragon lay coiled in the swampy muck beside a gigantic tree root, mist congealing around it. The only sound was chewing and squelching as it bit into the corpses floating past and sucked out their blood.

The dragon raised its head, a half-chewed corpse dangling from its mouth. Foam and gore oozed from its boulder-like teeth and dribbled into the murky water as bloated bodies drifted by.

Freya backed away. Nidhogg gulped down the corpse's leg and spat out the body.

'A little too chewy, that one,' it hissed. 'I like them fresh and bloody. By the time I get the battle-warriors they're a bit – drained. You, on the other hand . . .' Nidhogg leered at her. 'You look . . . very fresh. I've never had a live one before . . .' Drool dripped from its blood-speckled jaws as the dragon slowly uncurled himself from Yggdrasil's root and slithered towards her. His tail thrashed in the swamp, splattering her with bloody spray.

'Stop!' screamed Freya. 'You can't touch me! I'm a messenger from Asgard.'

Nidhogg paused. It ground its teeth together.

'Messenger?' it hissed. 'From the eagle? Where's the squirrel who always brings insults from him?'

'He couldn't make it, so I've come instead,' said Freya. She could hear her heart thudding against her chest. 'The message from the eagle is, "You smell worse than a thousand pigs."'

The dragon spat.

'Ha! I hope this means that revolting little squirrel is dead. Well, tell that stinking eagle from me that he is a coward and a – and a—'

Nidhogg paused.

'A what?' prompted Freya. She prayed Thor that the monster would not sense her heart pounding.

'It's a very long time since that piece of vermin last sent an insult,' said Nidhogg. 'I'm a little out of practice.'

'How about "You're a stinking son of a featherless freak"?' said Freya.

Nidhogg considered.

'Good insult,' he said. Freya tried not to look at the mashed-up guts and bones filling the dragon's gory mouth. 'What else have you got?' he mumbled, swallowing.

'May all your teeth fall out except one, and may that one have a cavity,' said Freya.

The dragon cackled. 'A curse *and* a jest. I like it. That'll teach that stinking bird dropping to taunt me. More.'

'You've got the head of a chicken and the courage of a sheep,' said Freya.

'More,' rasped Nidhogg, reaching out and ripping open another corpse with a horrible squelch.

'Leeches should drink you dry.'

'May you grow a wooden tongue.'

'May your children peck you to death.'

'May crows feast on your liver and your brain dry up.'

'May your wings drop off.'

'May fire burn your home and everyone in it.'

'May your eyes pop out of your head and blind your children.'

Freya paused.

'I like you better than Ratatosk,' said the dragon.

'He only *delivered* messages.'

'Don't forget,' said Freya. 'You don't have to stick with calling that eagle stinking. There's Woofy. Poofy. Smelly. Odoriferous. Pongy. Reeking. Whiffy. Rancid . . . uhhh . . . Poo-face.'

Nidhogg snatched up another corpse. Freya tried not to look.

'I'll remember,' said the dragon, crunching. 'Oy! Where are you going?' he hissed, as Freya started to edge away.

'I need to get back to Asgard,' said Freya.

'You're not going anywhere,' snapped Nidhogg, lurching towards her.

Freya stamped her foot. The dragon looked startled.

'The sooner I go, the sooner I can bring you the eagle's reply, remember?' said Freya.

'Hmmmm,' said the dragon. Bits of corpse dropped from his jaws.

'That is, if that tiny bird brain can think of anything to top your cleverness, which I very much doubt,' she added, trying to keep her voice strong.

Nidhogg retreated back into his swamp and grabbed a body.

'Come again soon,' said Nidhogg, chomping. 'And bring more insults.'

'Will do,' said Freya. She suddenly found she could breathe again.

She smiled to herself. She'd forgotten to tell him her favourite, 'May you grow like a carrot with your head in the ground.'

She'd save it for next time.

Freya stood tiny before the black walls and bolted, massive iron gates which protected Hel's poisonous hall. The ghosts streamed through; she was stuck. She reached out and touched the icy gate, recoiling at its oily chill. Somewhere in the dark distance she heard the mad howling of a ferocious dog. She looked up. The walls were far, far higher than she had realised.

There was only one way in.

Freya shook out her falcon skin, and flew silently over the massive Carrion-Gate of Hel's walled stronghold. Her body felt more at ease as a falcon now, she no longer feared that she would fall out of the air.

She perched for a moment on top of the wall to look over Hel's grisly hall. The only sound was hissing. Freya suddenly saw that the roof was thatched with writhing snakes.

It was now or never. Freya flew down and resumed her human shape.

Hel's door was open. Freya walked into the rain-damp citadel.

The cavernous hall teemed with the dead. Rotting faces, putrid bodies, half skeleton, half flesh, mingled with long-dead wraiths and ghosts, flitting and flickering. Corpses packed together on the low benches against the wet stone walls, huddling in the dark. Others roamed the vast emptiness, seeking Freya knew not what. The benches clogged with the dead stretched far into the distance, further than Freya could see.

Chandeliers criss-crossed with bones and skulls dangled from the roof, filled with unlit candles. Sconces made of skulls hung on the walls. There was a stone hearth in the centre. When Freya looked more closely, she saw that the cold fireplace was circled with teeth. There was no sign of Loki.

To the right of the door, the High Seat was empty. Behind it lay a curtained-off area.

Freya sat on a bench near the entrance, watching and waiting. There's no point in hiding, she thought. I want Hel to know I'm here.

Dead faces without number turned to stare at her. Wraiths, bodies, corpses, decomposed and mouldering, thousands and thousands and thousands, noiseless and prowling. There was an eerie silence as the teeming dead moved restlessly through the hall. The only sound was the *ssss ssss sssss* of the snakes writhing on the roof. Their poison dripped down the walls.

A hideous corpse leaned towards her and offered her a drinking horn. Freya sniffed it and recoiled. The horn was full of pee. The corpse opened its rotted mouth, laughed soundlessly and passed on.

'Where can I find Hel?' asked Freya.

'Talking to me?' said a corpse with a peeling face, scowling. 'Or to him?'

'Both,' said Freya.

'You know we can't speak unless we're spoken to,' said the corpse.

'Wouldn't bother talking to him, he's a right pain in the bum,' snapped the wraith.

'Bet you wish you still had a bum,' spat the corpse.

'Please tell me where Hel is,' Freya pleaded.

'She's lying on Sick-Bed, where else would she be?' said the wraith.

'Sick-Bed?' said Freya.

'Over there, look, behind the curtains. That's Hel's servant woman, Ganglot the Slow-Poke, coming over now,' said the corpse. 'Oy, you, budge up, you space hog, I was here first,' it said, grimacing hideously through what remained of its rotting green mouth and shoving its elbow through the bones of the skeletal body huddled beside it.

Freya saw an ancient woman dressed in rags walking towards her. Walking was actually the wrong word. Freya had never seen anyone move so slowly. She watched as the old woman crept nearer, inch by painful inch. Freya closed her eyes and rested her head for a moment in her ivory arms.

Ouch!

Someone was poking her in the shoulder. Freya woke.

Slowly, the old woman raised her arm and pointed to the curtained-off area. Freya followed her, but Ganglot's slow pace made her crazed. Time was what she did not have. Pushing past the snail-paced servant through the thronging shades, Freya went up to the filthy black curtains. The hangings were embroidered with many threads of black and grey, shot through with silver flecks. She looked more carefully, and saw that the ghastly curtains were decorated with pictures of gibbets, dangling with decomposing bodies. They stank of rot.

Do I knock? thought Freya. As she hesitated, a hand poked through the bed hangings and beckoned Freya inside.

Freya braced herself. Would Hel drip poison on her, or kill her with her foul breath? Would she be turned to stone when Hel revealed herself in all her hideousness?

Freya parted the heavy drapes, and entered.

She was in a small chamber, filled almost entirely by a bed hung with heavy black drapes, now drawn back. A young girl was lying there, eyes closed, a filthy blanket pulled up to her waist. Her wild, curly hair spread out everywhere on the pillow. Her skin was pale and plump. There was a strange, sickly-sweet smell in the room, as if something long-forgotten was rotting. An empty plate, dirty knife, and overturned goblet were scattered around her.

Freya looked about for the monster. Could this pink-cheeked girl be her daughter?

'I'm looking for Hel,' said Freya. 'I need to speak to her urgently.'

For a long moment, Freya thought the girl hadn't heard.

'Excuse me,' she said louder. 'I need to see Hel. Please, please, tell me where she is.'

'I – heard – you – the – first – time,' said the girl, pausing heavily between each word as if speaking was more than she could bear. Her pale eyelashes flickered.

Freya stared. This was Hel? This was the fearful Goddess who ruled the Underworld? This girl? She looked . . . she actually looked about Freya's age.

Hel spoke again. She sounded like someone who rarely spoke.

'Why – are – you – here – before – your – time?'

Freya poured out her story. She couldn't tell if Hel was listening or not.

'I know Loki is here somewhere. He stole Idunn. I must find her and bring her back to Asgard. The Gods are dying. The world is dying. I am dying.'

Hel smiled.

Freya held out her ivory arms. 'Help me.'

The blanket slipped and Freya glimpsed hideous, rotting blue flesh, mottled and oozing. She recoiled. Hel saw her face and tugged up the blanket.

'Not so pretty, am I?' she said. Her voice was harsh. 'I'm revolting, even to myself.'

Freya could think of nothing to say.

'Please help me,' said Freya again. 'I know—'

The entrance curtains parted, and Loki sauntered in. Freya drew in her breath. She hated him. She wanted to scratch out his strange eyes and beat him to death. He leered at her, then lounged at the foot of Hel's dank bed.

Hel didn't move. 'Yes, father?' Her pale eyes glittered like broken ice.

Loki smiled at her. His red and green eyes glistened.

'Looking good, girl.'

Hel scowled. 'You're not. And who said you could come into my bed closet?'

Loki laughed. 'I go where I please.'

'Not here you don't,' said Hel. 'This is *my* Hall. I built it. Hel is *my* kingdom. You're here because I allow it. Don't forget that.'

Loki's viper eyes flickered.

'Who's the pulse?' said Loki, jerking his thumb at Freya.

Hel smiled.

'The living all look alike to you?' she hissed. 'You know perfectly well who she is and why she's here.'

'Give me back Idunn!' shouted Freya. If only she could force him . . .

Loki ignored her.

'I'll show her out,' he said. 'You don't belong here.'

'You get out,' said Hel. 'Leave us alone. I don't often get to speak to someone with skin on their bones.'

'Aren't you Miss High and Mighty now?' said Loki. 'Don't let me interrupt your girl talk. But just remember, Hel, family loyalty is *everything*.'

Hel snorted. 'That's brilliant, coming from you. What have you ever done for me? Where were you when the Gods flung me here? You didn't lift a finger. You left Mum. You left us.'

'Oh stop whining,' said Loki.

'Where is Idunn?' demanded Freya. Her boldness no longer astonished her. After all, what did she have to lose?

'Safe.' He smirked.

'Everyone is dying because of you,' said Freya.

'Good,' said Loki. He fixed her with a piercing look. Freya shrank back. 'I know what my fate holds. A man's fate should be hidden, but I know mine. One day the Gods will catch me, bind me to three sharp stones with the guts of my own son, and a snake will drip poison on my face until the end of days. Drip. Drip. Drip. Who wouldn't do whatever they had to do, to avoid such a fate?'

Freya blanched. Put like that, Loki – almost – had a point. Then her heart hardened. If that was his fate, he had brought it upon himself.

'Bring Idunn back to Asgard,' said Freya. 'The Gods

will be grateful.'

'No chance,' said Loki.

'No one can avoid their fate,' said Freya.

Loki laughed. 'I've done pretty well so far. What luck I've had. I was disguised as Sleipnir, heading back to Skadi to get Idunn, when Woden's charm caught me and I was frozen, part of his sleeping army. But what great fortune! I stayed young while my enemies aged. And now I have Idunn.'

'But you're turning into ivory like the rest of us,' said Freya. 'Our time is running out.'

'That's where you're wrong, pulse. Look at yourself. Has your body become more ivory since you've been here?'

Freya peered quickly down her sweatshirt. Loki was right. The ivory had stopped just above her collarbone and hadn't spread any higher. The tops of her shoulders were still flesh-coloured.

'Woden's charms have no power here,' said Loki. 'And now that I have Idunn . . . I can wait.'

'But you're stuck in Hel,' said Freya, shuddering.

Loki shrugged. 'A lot better than being tied to a rock with poison splashing on your face. Don't you agree, daughter?'

Hel did not even bother to open her eyes.

Loki shook his head. 'And you were always such a chatty little girl,' he said.

'How would you know?' said Hel.

'All the Gods will be dead soon,' said Loki. 'And when they die Woden's charm will die with them. Then I'll return to Asgard and thwart my fate. I'm writing a new ending. No being chained to a rock with poison dripping on my face. And thanks to you, no troll hag stinking up the place. Just me. One God. One all-powerful, immortal God.'

'I hate the Gods,' said Hel. 'That doesn't mean I want *you* ruling, Dad.' She spat out the word *Dad* as if it contained bile. 'Now leave us alone and get out of my hall.'

Loki bowed. 'Whatever you say, queen of the dead,' he said. He edged round the bed and went to the chamber's entrance. Then he turned.

'What in the name of the accursed Gods do you think you're doing, you ugly little troll?' hissed Loki. His red and green eyes glared.

'I rule here, father.'

'Why not keep the mortal if you like her so much?'

Hel laughed her mirthless laugh.

'I can wait. Let her have her brief moment of light and warmth. Everyone ends up here in the end.' Hel turned over and faced the wall.

Loki slipped out.

Freya peeked round the curtains to see if he was waiting but Loki was gone.

Hel turned back slowly and looked at her.

'Will you help me?' said Freya.

Hel paused for such a long time Freya wondered if she had fallen asleep with her eyes open.

'How'd you like to spend eternity lying in a sick-bed hung with curtains called Glimmering Misfortune, and be waited on by two servants called Slow-Poke and Lazy Cow who move so slowly that they might as well be dead again because no one would notice?' said Hel, slowly raising herself to sit up. 'I never get out, I have no friends, in fact, everyone hates me, I have to spend my time with gangrenous, rotting raven food. I just lie here all day waiting for a cup of wine, then all night waiting for it to be removed. There is of course no day or night here, but I remember when I lived with my mother.

'I'm glad the Gods are dying. They kidnapped me when I was a child. They gagged my mother, tied her up, and took me back to Asgard. Not for long though. Woden threw my brother into the ocean – he was the world's biggest serpent, too bad he didn't bite Woden's

192

head off when he had the chance – then Woden took one look at me and hurled me down here, into this dark world below the worlds. You'll like it, he said, you'll be Queen down there. Look after all the dead people, the ones who've died of sickness and old age and fire. In other words, the ones he didn't want, the ones who were no use to him.

'Well, I don't like it. Not at all. So no, I won't help you. Now go away.'

Hel lay back down on Sick-Bed, and closed her eyes.

Freya stared at the angry pink-cheeked girl, her coiled snaky hair grey against her pale shoulders. She kept her eyes fixed on Hel's face, but they kept being drawn down to Hel's rotting, mouldering, foul-smelling dark-blue legs. Hel felt her staring, and yanked the curtains closed around her bed, shutting Freya out.

So that was that. It was over.

Freya bit her lip. She felt strangely light, as if all the thoughts in her head and feelings in her body had just evaporated. She'd failed. She'd always known she would, and yet, for a little while, she had dared to hope that somehow, in some way, having come so far, fate would reward her. She felt weirdly peaceful. She could fight her fate only so long. Somewhere far off she heard the hell-dog Garm howling.

I'd like to see Mum again one more time, thought Freya. She and Dad will never know what happened to me.

Tears filled her eyes. Angrily she rubbed them away.

The serving maid Ganglot waited silently by the threshold. Slowly she started to point to the exit.

A pale hand with cracked black nails poked through the tattered bed curtains.

'Wait,' said Hel.

Freya froze.

The hand beckoned her closer.

'Stay for a moment,' said Hel. 'Nice to look at someone who's still got skin on their face. Makes a change.'

Freya hesitated. Why should she spend a moment of the little time she had left with this hag?

Oh why not? thought Freya. Nothing matters now. Carefully, she sat on the edge of the musty bed. If she just looked at Hel's top half, she was more bearable.

Hel slowly reached over and picked up the empty gold plate lying on the mildewed blanket.

'See this plate?' said Hel. 'I named it Hunger. My knife is called Starving. I'm the only one who eats around here, so I thought that would be fitting. My goblet is called Thirst, bit of a joke, really, because I can wait all day for it to be filled . . .'

Freya shrugged.

'Do you like my bed hangings?' said Hel.

Freya shrugged again. She wasn't feeling very talkative.

'I went through so many names for them,' said Hel. She fingered the dark fabric. 'Rickets. Glittering Pain. Shining Harm. Shimmering Torment. They've been Glimmering Misfortune now for ages. I might rename them again in the next hundred years or so.'

'That'll be fun,' said Freya. She felt numb.

Hel looked at her with her ice-dead eyes.

'Are you laughing at me?'

'No,' said Freya. 'I like naming things too. I even named all my soft toys when I was little. I called my dog Bel Gazou.'

'I called mine Garm,' said Hel. 'That means rag. He's huge and ugly. Everything here is ugly.'

'You're not ugly,' said Freya.

Hel snorted.

'Not ugly? Are you blind? I'm a monster.'

Freya shook her head.

'You know,' said Freya, 'if you tied back your hair,

you'd look quite pretty.'

'Pretty?' said Hel. 'What's pretty?'

'It means . . . you look good,' said Freya.

Hel stared at her. 'How would I know?'

'Look.' Freya fumbled with her unruly curls and took off the tortoiseshell clip. 'May I touch your hair?'

Hel started as if Freya had asked if she could brand her.

'You want to . . . touch me?' she said.

'Well, your hair . . . I was going to . . .' Freya stopped in confusion. Maybe you died on the spot touching Hel. Her two servants Ganglati and Ganglot were still turning around. I'll be rotten by the time they finish, she thought.

'We both have Medusa hair,' said Freya.

'Who's Medusa?' said Hel.

'A monster from the Greek myths,' said Freya. 'She turned people to stone if they looked at her. She had snakes for hair.' Perhaps that wasn't the politest thing to say, thought Freya. In fact, how stupid could she be, telling a monster she looked like a monster?

Hel spat. 'A monster? People always like monsters in stories.'

'I thought you'd be old and ugly,' said Freya.

'I am old and ugly,' said Hel. 'I'm a rotting corpse.'

'Not all of you,' said Freya. 'When you tie back those curls you'll look quite pretty.'

Freya fumbled in her pocket. She had the feather, a piece of dirty tissue with some gum in it, the decoy nuts she'd never need now, and the shiny silver pot of pink lipgloss – Bubble Gum Burst – with a mirror. Freya looked at the gloss wistfully for a moment. She'd saved up for weeks to buy it.

'Put this on,' said Freya.

Hel looked at the burnished little pot and raised herself on to her elbow.

'What is it?' she asked. 'A jewel? Magic?'

'It's called lipgloss,' said Freya. 'It will make your mouth shine.' She opened the round pot and handed the gloss to Hel.

'I like shine,' said Hel. Then she gasped.

'There's – there's someone in here,' she whispered, pointing to her reflection in the tiny round mirror.

'That's you,' said Freya.

'Me?' said Hel. 'Me?' She gazed at her reflection, herself and not herself. 'Is that me? Is that really me? It can't be . . . I look . . . I look . . . my face . . .' She raised her hands to her face, and touched it, staring at herself in the little mirror.

'This is a great wonder, to see yourself so clear.' She

stuck out her tongue. Her reflection mirrored her. Hel smiled a tiny smile.

'Dip your finger in the gloss and smear it on your lips,' said Freya.

'You first,' hissed Hel. 'I don't want to be poisoned.'

Freya smeared her finger with pink gloss and rubbed it on her lips. Hel copied her. Then she looked at herself in the mirror and smiled.

'A new you,' said Freya. What a before-and-after picture Hel would make.

Hel's bony fingers gripped the pot.

'Keep it,' said Freya.

Hel was too busy looking at herself to reply. She dipped her fingers in the pot and smeared the gloss on her cheeks and forehead.

'I'm sorry,' said Freya. 'It must be horrible being here.'

'It is,' said Hel. 'It's hel.' She smiled grimly. 'I haven't always been here. I remember being with my mother Angrboda in a cave. My brothers were there too.'

'I'm an only child,' said Freya.

'Lucky you. My brothers were Fenrir the wolf and Jormungand the snake. Try fighting over who gets the biggest piece of meat with them.'

Hel gazed at the lipgloss.

'A great gift like this deserves recompense,' she said. 'Ganglot! Fetch the *eski* under my bed.'

Hel was giving her a gift. Freya dreaded to think what it would be. A dead snake? A bone strung on a necklace? Nail shavings?

Freya took the wooden box from the sepulchral servant and opened it. She adjusted her face to look grateful for whatever horror it contained.

Inside was a nut.

Freya gripped it tight. Her heart stopped. She swallowed.

'I'm doing this for you,' said Hel. 'Not for them. I hate the Gods. I'll always hate them. But my revenge can wait until the Axe-Age and the Wind-Age and the Wolf-Age at the bitter end of days.'

Freya clasped the nut carefully in one hand, and took out her falcon feather with the other.

'I'll build a shrine to you,' said Freya.

'That will be a first,' said Hel. 'Don't think you'll get too many worshippers.'

'Goodbye,' said Freya. 'Thank you. I'll never forget you.'

'Stay,' said Hel suddenly. 'You'll never make it back to Asgard alive. You're already ivory up to your neck. Here you can live forever. Just think, mortal Freya, life everlasting. Your friends and family will all be here to join you soon enough.'

Freya hesitated.

'This place isn't so bad once you get used to it,' said Hel, slowly sitting up. 'Everyone's here, you know. All the greats. You can meet anyone you like. There's no pain. No suffering.'

Freya's head swam. She could have immortality — of a sort — or a tiny chance of getting back to Asgard alive before fate turned her into a chess piece and a living death asleep for eternity.

She breathed the fetid air and stared at the sad girl looking up at her so hopefully.

'I can't,' said Freya. 'I have to try.'

'Go then,' said Hel. 'See if I care.'

Freya slipped through the bed hangings on to the threshold and back into the hall, reaching into her pocket for the nuts she had brought. She looked around for Loki, but couldn't see him amongst the whirling dead. Quickly, she pushed through the teeming ghosts, flinging on the falcon skin, and flew through the open door into the murky gloom outside Hel's hall.

A man guarded the doorway. Loki.

He's not expecting me to fly, thought Freya. At that

moment, Loki raised his eyes and saw her.

He snarled with rage and sprang up at her. Freya hurled herself into the air, flying high over the gates. Behind her she could hear pounding feet as Loki turned into Sleipnir and jumped after her. She felt his hot breath as the horse leapt into the air, swiping at her with his flailing hooves.

She twisted away from him and flew higher through the foggy mist.

Loki snarled with rage. 'Thjazi will get you!' he bellowed. 'I'll soon be picking apart your carrion!'

Freya's heart thudded as she flew ever higher up and up into the blackness, Loki's curses ringing after her, then she was once again inside Hekla and whirling upwards, the prize clutched in her right claw.

9 Asgard

Freya flew out of Hekla. After the endless gloom of Hel, the bright sunlight almost blinded her. She looked down and saw Snot's ripped and torn body, sprawled on the blackened lava by the volcano's mouth.

Roskva was nowhere to be seen.

'Snot!' Freya wailed.

He'd died for her. But she had to leave him behind. Darting through the smoky ash she soared into the clear sky above the black volcanoes. She was on her own. She would have to find Asgard on her own.

Stay calm, she told herself, stay calm. Just head for

the mountains. You can do this.

And then she saw him. He was a dot on the horizon, then a blot in the sky, growing larger and larger every second. And he was coming straight at her.

Freya flew for her life. Over the barren wilderness, high over the mountains, Freya flew. But every time she twisted her head the giant eagle was a little bit closer. An eagle can outfly a falcon, she thought, despairingly.

All too soon, Freya heard the whoosh whoosh of frantic wings, ripping the air. Glancing round, she saw the huge eagle hurtling after her, filling the sky.

Her world shrank to a pinprick of straining muscles, pounding heart and beating wings. Faster! Faster! Faster! Faster! Faster!

Freya heard a terrible whirr as the monstrous eagle closed in, talons outstretched, ready to rip her apart.

She felt the air hum. Thjazi was her death, and it was almost upon her.

NO! She dived steeply, twisting away from his talons. Then she opened her left claw, and let a nut fall.

The eagle spiralled after the nut, plummeting towards the ground. Freya flew harder and faster, tearing the clouds, straining to get as far ahead as possible before Thjazi discovered he didn't have Idunn.

On and on she flew, terror and panic jolting her to ever-greater speed. Had she gone in the right direction? Where was Asgard? Why, why, did she never know where she was? She'd followed Alfi's instructions, she was sure she'd followed—

And there it was. Yggdrasil, the world tree, shooting up into the blue sky before her. Freya zoomed towards it.

But behind her was Thjazi, and the *whirr-whirr-whirr* of his wings bearing down on her.

Freya thought of her PE teacher, mean Miss Sylvester, bellowing at her to run faster in the school cross-country race. Freya had been so terrified she'd run like a crazed animal and wound up on the cross-country team.

Freya veered and flew straight for Yggdrasil. Go! Go! Go!

She shrieked, as the high walls of Asgard towered into view. She could see two specks, which turned into people, which turned into . . . Alfi and Roskva. They were standing on either side of what looked like a gigantic pile of kindling and wood.

The eagle was now so close behind she heard his giant wings slice the air.

He'll get me here, thought Freya. I'll fly over the

wall and he'll come straight after me. There is no escape. How could I have thought I could escape him? He'll rip me to pieces when I land. Oh Gods!

'Light the fire!' screamed Alfi.

Fire? thought Freya.

Flames whooshed high into the air. She felt the heat singe her feathers like a hot furnace, Thjazi only a few hair's-breadths behind her. Freya spun out of the sky into the citadel of the Gods, clutching the nut, reeling to avoid the fireball.

Thjazi was following too fast and flew straight through the flames. She heard a terrible agonised scream as his wings caught fire.

Twisting in agony, the eagle fell to earth, in a thrashing burning heap.

Freya lay on the ground inside the walls, gasping and trembling. Dimly she saw Alfi and Roskva stabbing the flaming, shrieking eagle. His death cries tore through her.

There was a horrible smell of blood and burnt, smoking feathers.

'He's dead! He's dead!' they shouted. Then Roskva and Alfi ran up to her. Their faces were ivory to the tips of their white-streaked hair.

Freya flung off the falcon skin and regained human

form. She lay panting and shivering, gulping the air through her singed lungs. The nut was clutched in her ivory hand. Roskva had to prise open her fingers before she would release Idunn.

The All-Father stumbled over to them. Roskva held out the great prize.

Woden sighed and took hold of the nut, cradling it in his bony, palsied grip. Tears poured from his eye. He murmured runes, again and again, shaking his head and trembling, his face scrunched with effort, his eye bulging. The other Gods staggered over, spectre-grey, muttering and murmuring, hissing and whispering.

Oh, get it right, prayed Freya, get it right.

Suddenly a girl stood before them, golden and shimmering. Over her arm she carried a basket. She smiled, and held out an apple.

Woden took a bite, and then another. His twisted limbs began to straighten, and tufts of hair fuzzed on his bald scalp.

Freya's body tingled. She looked down and saw the ivory recede from her arms and legs. Roskva and Alfi were leaping and whooping, ivory no more. Above her, Yggdrasil's mighty branches sprouted leaves, wreathing the sky.

Idunn walked silently amongst the reviving Gods,

smiling and radiant, passing each an apple from her basket. The Gods snatched them and ate greedily, crying and laughing as they saw flesh gradually returning to their withered limbs and colour flecking their sunken cheeks.

Idunn smiled at Freya.

'Enjoy your youth, mortal,' she whispered.

There was a roaring and bellowing as a gigantic grey-bearded man picked up a hammer and tried to swing it over his head before gasping and letting it drop. 'Ooofff, my aching arms,' he moaned. 'That thing weighs more than a whale.'

'Council of the Gods to meet NOW by the Well of Urd,' Woden boomed. The heavens shook. 'We need to trick some giants into re-building our Halls.' Then he groaned and clutched his thigh. 'Ooh, my lumbago. Idunn, I want more apples NOW!'

There was a happy buzz as the Immortals hobbled to their ancient meeting place, laughing and tossing their wisps of hair. Their bodies eased and lengthened as Freya gazed after them.

Is that it? thought Freya.

The Goddess Frigg paused.

'I almost forgot,' she rasped, holding out her liver-spotted hand, 'my falcon skin.'

Silently Freya handed it back to her.

Frigg shook out the silky feathers and examined them. 'They're singed,' she shrieked. She clicked her tongue against her tooth and sighed loudly. 'Why weren't you more careful?'

'I did—'

'You'd better keep it,' said Frigg, handing it back. 'I can't fly around in *that*. I'll use Freyja's.'

The Goddess Freyja glared at her.

'I don't have my falcon skin any more,' she snapped. 'Like an idiot I loaned it to Loki long ago, remember?'

'It's hanging at Skadi's,' said Freya.

The Goddess tossed her thickening white hair, touched with gold, and scowled.

'You left it there?' said Freyja. 'Idiot.'

'If you remember,' said Freya, 'we were trying to find Idunn.'

Frigg linked arms with Freyja. 'We'll get it back,' said Frigg. 'Let's raise the matter at the Council.'

'Idunn!' shouted Freyja. 'More apples! I still have bingo wings!'

'Apples are hard to eat without teeth,' grumbled Frigg.

The two Goddesses tottered off together after Idunn, propping each other up. Only Woden stayed behind, lost in thought, his brow furrowed. The two ravens on his shoulders fluttered with newly-sprouted feathers.

'You did well, Freya,' said Roskva. She nodded. 'You did well. We owe you – everything.'

Freya beamed. Her body ached all over.

'Whose idea – the fire?' she rasped.

'Mine,' said Alfi. He grinned. 'Thjazi chased me, I barely got away from him, and I thought you'd suffer the same fate. Roskva wasn't here, she only just made it back, I had to think for myself. I realised we had to do something to stop Thjazi if he flew here after you . . .'

Roskva scowled. 'And why do you think I sent you here ahead of me?'

'Fair enough,' said Alfi.

'I'd hardly have a reputation for wisdom if I couldn't see further into the future than *you*,' said Roskva.

Alfi snorted. 'What reputation for wisdom?'

They smiled at one another.

'I could have been burnt to a crisp,' said Freya.

'But you weren't,' said Roskva.

'Roskva! Alfi! I need you *now!*' bellowed Thor.

'We'd better go,' said Alfi.

'Business as usual,' said Roskva.

'Snot?' said Freya.

Roskva's face fell. 'Thjazi attacked. I managed to run away, but Snot . . .'

'I hope the All-Father will send the Choosers of the Slain to bring him back here,' said Alfi.

Freya gasped. 'That reminds me,' she said.

She ran up to Woden and tugged on his sleeve.

'I must know,' she said. 'What will happen to the others?'

'Must?' he said, glaring down at her. 'Must? Must? What others?'

'The chess pieces we left behind. In the museum? The sleeping army?'

'Their time will come, when the forces of darkness rise up at the fated end of days and another world begins,' he murmured.

'There afterwards will be found in the shining grass
Wondrous chess pieces
Treasures which the Gods possessed in ancient times,'
he recited.

'. . . and until then?' said Freya.

'They sleep,' said the All-Father. He fixed her with his piercing single eye.

'Why are you still here?' said Woden. 'Asgard is forbidden to mortals. Alfi! Take her to Bifrost. Hornblower, go home.' And he staggered off to join the others, straightening up little by little as he drifted away, becoming more and more the All-Seeing, All-Powerful, All-Father again with every step.

Freya stood. The Gods had already forgotten her. Well, what did she expect? A crown? A gold arm ring? Thanks?

Freya heard shouting and the clank of metal. Asgard's newly green meadows suddenly gleamed with shields and swords as heavily armoured fighters jousted and clashed, laughing as they died.

'Woden's warriors fight again in their playground,' said Alfi. 'There will be feasting tonight in Valhalla when they all come back to life.'

'And tomorrow?' said Freya.

'They fight and kill each other all over again,' said Alfi. 'And so on, and so on, until the end of days.'

'Out of my way, you stinking son of a mare!' bellowed a familiar voice as a giant Bear-Man thundered across the battlefield, wildly swinging his sword. 'I'll rip out your guts and stuff them in your face!'

'Snot?' said Freya. 'Snot? Snot!' she screamed.

The Bear-Man paused for a fraction of a second and raised his sword, saluting them. Then he charged back into battle.

'The Valkyries fetched him,' said Freya. 'I'm glad.'

She breathed deeply, drawing in Asgard's faint perfume of fresh grass and honey and sun-dried linens.

Alfi walked her to Bifrost across the flower-filled meadows. There was too much to say, and nothing to say.

'Well . . .' said Freya.

'Well . . .' said Alfi.

'What will happen to you now?' asked Freya.

Alfi shrugged. 'Wallop giants with Thor, watch out for Loki, dodge flying bones in Valhalla. Skadi will want vengeance for her father . . .'

'Same old,' said Freya.

'Same old,' said Alfi. 'Is that what people say now?'

'Yeah,' said Freya.

'I have a lot of catching up to do,' he said.

They stood on the edge of Bifrost, flames leaping around them.

'Will I ever see you again?' said Freya.

'If that is our fate,' said Alfi.

She hugged him. 'I hope it is.'

'Me too,' said Alfi. 'Here. Take this.'

He handed her an arm bracelet, heavy with gold. 'From my Master,' he said. 'And this,' he added, offering her an intricately carved brooch, 'this is from me.'

Freya beamed and took the jewellery. Then she saw

his grave face.

'Will you be all right?' said Freya. 'Do you have friends here?'

'I quite like Woden's ravens,' said Alfi after a long pause. 'And the wolves . . . after they've been fed.'

'No one else?' said Freya.

Alfi shook his head. 'Just Roskva.'

Did a sister count as a friend?

'We'd be friends if I lived in Asgard or you lived in London,' said Freya suddenly.

Alfi smiled. 'We would,' he said. 'And I'll remember that, always.'

He was there, and then he wasn't.

Freya unbuckled Snot's bear-skin cloak and left it lying on the ground. Then she set off on the long walk down Bifrost, alone.

London and the Thames stretched out before her, oblivious to the flaming bridge above it. London, crisp and shining in the sunlight, had never looked so beautiful.

Freya stumbled off the Gods' rainbow road. Her feet touched the hard surface of the Millennium Bridge and she jostled the horde of French schoolchildren hurrying to the Tate Modern, pointing at her and jabbering.

Freya exhaled deeply. She'd been to Hel and back. She'd escaped giants, fled fire, outwitted dragons. She'd been terrified and half-drowned and near death.

And now, thank Gods, it was over. She could go back to her normal, boring life, shuttling between her parents, losing her gym kit, and being told off for leaving her junk all over the kitchen.

How wonderful.

Freya smiled and switched on her mobile.

Beep. Beep. Beep. Beep. Beep.

Her phone was filled with messages. She clicked it open.

'Uhhh . . . Dad?' said Freya.

10 London

Light bulbs flashed. 'Freya! Over here! Freya! Smile! Freya! Freya! Freya!'

All around her journalists and onlookers and photographers swarmed on to the Millennium Bridge, pushing and shoving and shouting questions at her. Where had they all come from? She'd only just spoken to her dad, and he'd yelled: 'Wait there! Don't move. We're coming! Just stay on the phone with me . . .' and then her battery had died and she was standing on the bridge leaning against the side watching the boats and thinking of nothing when she was suddenly surrounded.

217

'Did you steal the chessmen?' 'Who kidnapped you?' 'Who stole the chessmen?' 'Was that you with those kids in fancy dress?' 'Where'd they take you?' 'Why'd you run away?' 'Where've you been hiding?' 'Where are the chess pieces now?'

Freya shrank back under the barrage of questions, blinking at the flashing, clicking cameras, the noise, the honking cars and the hustling-bustling scrum of people arguing and thrusting phones at her.

'We'll BUY your story — don't give it away!' screamed a bald man waving a cheque book.

'He's a crook — talk to us, Freya!' shrieked a woman with black, lacquered, swept-up hair.

Everywhere she turned there were more and more people yelling and gabbling into microphones. Freya heard odd snatches — 'horse', 'looks a right mess', 'Runaway or victim — you decide!' Camera crews pulled up, blocking traffic, followed by an ice-cream van.

Three police cars, sirens wailing, screeched to a halt.

Through a tiny gap in the jostling crowd Freya saw her parents' faces pressed against the back window of the middle car. Then they started waving frantically.

'MUM! DAD!' she screamed, struggling to get to them.

Clare burst from the car and shoved her way

through the mob. Bob followed. Two police officers, an older man and a younger woman with dark brown hair pulled back into a ponytail, shouldered their way towards her.

'It's all right, Freya, we'll take over from here,' yelled the policewoman. 'I'm Sunil, and I'll be looking after you.'

Clare pushed past Sunil and flung her arms around Freya.

'Thank Woden! Thank Thor!' said Clare, clutching her. 'Praise Njord! You're safe!'

'Freya! My Gods, Freya, where have you been?' shouted Bob, trying to hug her as well.

The cameras snapped frantically.

'I've been to Asgard and Jotunheim and Hel. I've met the Gods. I've saved them, and I've saved the world,' she thought, then suddenly realised she'd spoken out loud. She covered her open mouth with her hand.

'Concussed,' she heard Sunil murmur to her parents. 'We'll take her straight to Baldr's hospital to be checked out before interviewing her.'

'And a bath,' muttered Clare.

'Are you arresting her?' shouted a reporter.

'Everyone get back,' ordered the policeman. He pulled out his radio.

'Am I in trouble?' said Freya.

'Don't say anything. We're getting a lawyer. It will be fine,' said Clare, hugging her again. She tightened her fingers on Freya's bruised arm. Freya winced.

'Get out of the way please,' said Clare. 'My daughter needs to rest,' she added firmly. 'She doesn't know who stole the chessmen, and she will be making a full statement to the police. Now move.'

'Come on, leave her alone, we'll hold a press conference later at Snowhill Street Station,' said the policeman. 'Back off, show's over, move along.' He guided them into the back seat of the first police car and slammed the door.

Freya sat between Bob and Clare as Sunil drove off. She leaned her head back and slumped. Someone else was in charge. Someone else was making decisions for her. She felt a great sense of relief.

Bob put his arm around her shoulder. Clare clutched her hand. Will they pull me apart? thought Freya.

'Freya,' whispered Bob, glancing at Sunil to make sure she couldn't hear, 'I saw something . . . odd the night you vanished.'

'What?' said Freya.

'I saw you . . . spinning through the air with the chess pieces. And then you – and they – vanished. I know it sounds crazy, but that's what I saw.'

Clare rolled her eyes.

'Shut up, Bob,' said Clare. 'One of the great joys of being divorced from you is that I get to ignore rubbishy statements like that.'

'Well, Freya?' said Bob.

Freya reached into her pocket and touched the falcon feather, the arm band, and Alfi's brooch.

'Dad,' whispered Freya. 'It's a long saga.'

Acknowledgements

I'd like to thank Andrew Franklin of Profile Books, and Stephen Page of Faber, for inviting me to write whatever I liked, an enticing and irresistible offer. Andrew also stopped me when we were discussing possible ideas to point out that there might be a book in the Lewis Chessmen.

I'm extremely grateful to Professor Eric Stanley, Professor Mary Clayton, and Dr Emily Lethbridge, who kindly cast aside all scholarly reticence and answered endless questions about what a non-Christian world based on the Anglo-Saxon and Norse gods might be like.

This book would never have been written without the help and encouragement of my wonderful writer friends Steven Butler and Emily Woof. My special thanks to Steven for asking for the first paragraph as his birthday present, and for being my first reader, and to Emily for the world-shattering suggestion that

Christianity never happened.

I'd also like to thank Rosemary Sandberg, Martin Stamp and Joshua Stamp-Simon for thoughtful comments and good cheer.

Anyone who wants to find out more about the Norse gods must read Kevin Crossley-Holland's brilliant, poetic re-telling in *The Penguin Book of Norse Myths*.

The Lewis Chessmen are still sleeping in the British Museum and the National Museum of Scotland.